Sam

and the

Stolen Words

Toni Bunnell

www.tonibunnell.com

First published in 2014 by Toni Bunnell, York, UK

www.tonibunnell.com

ISBN: 978-1-78280-318-8

© Toni Bunnell 2014

A CIP record for this book is available from the British Library.

Printed and bound in Great Britain by
Apple Print and Creative Ltd, Newbury, Berkshire

Cover / text design and photographs by Toni Bunnell

www.tonibunnell.com

SAMUEL AND THE STOLEN WORDS

Toni Bunnell was born in Manchester and now lives in York, after a few years in Heidelberg, Germany. She is a singer-songwriter, musician, broadcaster, hedgehog rehabilitator and a wildlife biologist.

ALSO BY TONI BUNNELL

Music Makes a Difference*

The Room Between the Floorboards

A Door in Time

The Fidgit

Tales of Sweeper Joe the Hero

A Life Well Lived

The Disappearing Hedgehog*

ebook available for all except*

www.tonibunnell.com

For Jake and Cassie

May you always follow your dreams and
continue to dwell within the pages of books

Chapter One

Into the book

Samuel climbed inside the book, folding back the pages neatly. With outstretched fingers he reached out and straightened every corner. With tenderness and care he smoothed flat the ivory pages that spread around him in every direction. Night was upon him and, as usual, the book welcomed him with open arms and not a little sense of nostalgia. It had missed Samuel. During the long daylight hours when no touch lit upon its pages, caressed its spine, held it wonderingly to the light to dwell further on the fascinating inscription inside the cover, Samuel had been missed.

These days he alone took notice of the book and cared for it. His fingers would linger on the embossed cover with the main characters depicted in colour and high relief. He would close his eyes and slowly draw his fingertips over the figures. Sight was not needed to begin to know them, to learn a little about the lives they would lead inside the book, once the pages had been turned. Tonight Samuel was too tired for reading.

Cocooned inside the book he entered the world of dreams. Through a chink in the curtains in his room the book could be seen lying on the wooden table beside a child's bed. The bed was empty. Samuel was inside the book.

Morning brought shafts of sunlight glinting through the window panes and a sense of anticipation. Today Samuel would be getting a puppy. He slid sideways from the pages of the book and dropped a little awkwardly onto the pillow of his bed. The bed that lay crisp and clean and unslept in. No dent disturbed the firmly drawn-across sheets with their hospital corners. No imprint of a small body could be found underneath the eiderdown. The bed was as pristine as his mother had left it the day before when she had changed the sheets and pillow case.

As always she had marvelled at how clean and unwrinkled the bedding on her son's bed appeared despite, unknown to her, his best efforts to make it look as if it had been slept in. It was as if he weighed no more than half a bag of sugar, or a halfpence worth of rice, so lightly did his body impact the sheets, so little did he seem to move about in the night. She had put this down to the fact that Samuel, although now aged eight, was small for his age, weighed little more than a feather and slept a dreamless sleep. The sleep of the innocent.

Her eyes were temporarily drawn to the book that lay, unopened, on the bedside table. A passing glance only, with merely a mental note that Samuel didn't appear to be reading much these days. She could not have known the truth, the truth that was stronger than anything she might have imagined. Samuel spent little time perusing the pages and stories that lay within the book. He had no need to. He had met the characters. He slept inside the book.

Chapter 2

A world apart

Samuel sat at his school desk. His pen dipped in and out of the inkwell set into the right hand corner. Slowly and painstakingly he drew spidery letters on the page that lay before him. Pristine white paper that had never been touched by a pen or pencil and was now changing as the words began to flourish.

Like frost spreading across glass as a wintry night took hold, the letters gradually appeared, linking up to form words that, in turn, grew into sentences. Sentences that held meaning for Samuel, that told a story, a tale of sorts; revealed a small part of the life that was Samuel's. A life short in the living, simple in shape and form, not particularly remarkable, but unique nevertheless. For this life belonged to Samuel and Samuel alone.

The day had started out foggy and Samuel had only been able to make out rough outlines of trees on his journey to school. The ground had cracked under his feet as he made his way cautiously to the car. His mother held the door for him and waited patiently until he was in his seat with his bag at his feet.

'Don't forget your seat belt Samuel,' she reminded him. Samuel nodded. The reminder, no longer needed these days, came without fail. The words no longer irritated him. In fact he barely heard them, unnecessary as they were. He had fastened his belt automatically and now gazed out of the window as they flew along.

Vision did not come easily to Samuel. He could decipher shapes, but only with some difficulty, depending on the level of light available to him and the context of his surroundings. Places he knew well were easy to recognise. He could find his way round anywhere that was familiar to him. The classroom was well lit and the morning was going well.

This was Samuel's favourite lesson. Writing. The teacher often gave them a prompt such as 'I arrived at school today to find....' or 'A letter came in the post today. It said.....' He enjoyed the prompts but mostly did not need them and liked to allow his imagination to take him where it wished. To draw him in and along an unexplored path and to introduce him to characters he had never previously met.

Today he was writing freely and was in his element, drawn inside a story of his own making. So engrossed was he that he did not hear the firm words of the teacher asking them all to stop writing. It was only as she stood over his desk, and blocked the light from the window, that Samuel realised that he was in the classroom and that the writing must stop.

Mrs Walters, the teacher, was by no means strict but it was her ardent wish that all her charges should have some level of discipline. This was important in order for them to be able to structure their days, level control over what they did and lead satisfying lives in the community. Above all she wanted her pupils to be self-sufficient and out-going; confident in all they did.

Samuel had no real need for a guide dog as he had reasonable residual vision and was able to manoeuvre round objects fairly well in good light conditions. Once dusk came, however, it was a different story. He was less confident, more visually challenged and more likely to stumble over unforeseen objects in his path.

****

Ben was a dog that shone from the start. The first born of six puppies, he was eager to explore and curious in the extreme. However, it soon became obvious to the breeder that he was not thriving as he might and would not make the expected height for a Labrador. After brief negotiations with Samuel's parents they agreed on a reduced price. Ben was placed in Samuel's arms and the two installed in the back of the car, the safety belt going round the pair of them.

'Just in case of an accident,' said Samuel's father, Toby, and: 'Just for today he can travel with you. After that he goes in the back.' Samuel nodded silently, his eyes gleaming with happiness and love for a dog that, until an hour ago, he had never even set eyes upon. The engine kicked into life as Sarah, his mother, turned the key and, glancing at her husband beside her, they set off for home, the precious cargo secured in the back seat.

****

Samuel liked to run with the wind. In an open space, where he could come to no harm, he would close his eyes tightly and twirl round and round in a circle, moving faster and faster. Arms stretched out by his sides he loved to feel the pressure of the cool air against his exposed hands and face as he rapidly changed direction. He tried to catch the wind unawares when, in fact, it was catching him. It turned his little body from side to side as it wished until, eventually, Samuel, or the wind, subsided.

Some days, when the wind was particularly strong, Samuel would find a small hilly knoll to stand upon. He would position himself so that he was facing into the mouth of the wind then, as it built up strength, he would leap into the air and it would carry him a short distance. For the brief moment, seconds only, that Samuel was airborne, he truly felt as if he was flying, as if he belonged to another world where perfect vision was not necessarily something to strive for. He felt himself to be safe and secure and able to embark on an adventure. And at night, safely installed inside the book, that was precisely what Samuel was able to do. Go on a voyage of discovery.

Stars lit the evening sky. It was the time of night when Samuel would draw back the curtains slightly and peer out into the blackness. The house lay on the edge of town, bordering the moors, with a small wood to the rear. Light pollution had no place here and the stars shone in all their splendour with no haze from neighbouring houses or street lights to obscure them.

When Samuel closed his eyes he could see the pattern of the stars imprinted on the inside of his eyelids. Often, when the desire to draw overwhelmed him, he would commit the stars to paper, carefully positioning each pinprick of light as he remembered it. Once the stars had taken the form of ink dots on the page, Samuel would raise the dots using a pin, so that he could feel the pattern of the stars underneath his fingers and had no further need to gaze at the page in order to recall them.

Samuel was a boy of many parts. Gregarious and a social recluse by turns, he was something of an enigma. He liked hours of solitude, during which he would let his mind wander freely, letting it loose to its own imaginings. His mother referred to his tendency for leaving a conversation as 'zoning out'.

Even when he was amongst others, and apparently engaging with what was happening, he would suddenly switch off. His ability to do this was a source of utmost irritation for others around him but a gift sent from heaven for Samuel. Whenever he felt the conversation becoming too difficult, or attention towards him too excessive, he would vanish entirely from the room, if not in person, then certainly in spirit.

Often, when Samuel was 'absent without leave' he was 'in the book'. The book that could only truly encapsulate him at night time when the shadows drew in and, to all intents and purposes, he was granted leave of absence as he was thought to be asleep.

But it was only at these times that Samuel was truly awake. Once absorbed within the book he took on a new persona. Instead of being Samuel, the 'small for his age' boy who struggled with some of his lessons, had difficulty making out shapes in dim light, and was less than forthcoming when asked to express his thoughts during a lesson, he became an intrepid explorer. Instilled with confidence, and with his spirits bolstered, he would tread the pages of the book with purposefulness and determination. Once inside the book Samuel became a different person.

Chapter 3
The whisper

It began as a whisper. An almost imperceptible sense of knowing that threaded its way through the book. Like a finger tracing a pattern on a frosted pane of glass, the whisper moved across the pages. Following no particular path it traversed line after line on the printed page. When it reached the colour plates, which were protected from the light and rough fingers by a thin layer of translucent paper, it traced the edges of each character depicted in the picture.

Every living thing was touched by the light finger of the tracing whisper. As the whisper flowed over the pages the characters began to glow with anticipation and the book was brought to life. The whisper became more than a whisper. It grew to murmurings. A brief message being passed on by word of mouth from one character to another throughout the book.

'Samuel's back. He's inside the book!'

****

Samuel had discovered his ability to enter the world of books by accident. Engrossed in reading a chapter from the book on his bedside table he had allowed his thoughts to wander. As one thought followed another he moved further and further into the lives of the characters until he was no longer just following their story, held within the lines of the book, he was following their lives after the lines of the story had run out. Samuel had moved beyond the words and had entered the story.

He was vaguely aware that not all of his body was still lying on his bed in the little room that held it. Part of him was physically inside the book. The further he reached out to the characters, the further inside the book he moved, until eventually he was immersed totally in the book, in every sense of the word.

Parents, wanting their children to help with housework, or to get on with their homework, often tell them 'get your head out of that book.' Were they to look more closely they would be shocked to see that their child's head had literally vanished inside the book. A few sharp words, at an opportune, or inopportune (depending on your point of view) moment had often served to avert a potential disaster.

Some children vanished from their rooms while reading a book, never to be seen again.

Some children reappeared the next day, to cross words and a strict telling off from their parents who assumed that their child had run away without a word of warning and had merely returned on a whim. The truth, had they listened to it, was stronger than fiction.

Samuel had perfected the art of entering and leaving the world of story at will. To be precise, the story held within one particular book. The book that lay day in and day out on his bedside table. It was his escape from the exacting world of homework and necessity and his escape into the beguiling world of fantasy and make-believe.

Samuel trod the stairs to his bedroom, clutching Ben, his puppy, firmly to his chest. Occasionally, his foot missed the carpet runner that snaked up the central part of the stairs and he tripped slightly on the brass pin that held the carpet firmly in place at the sides. Ben was heavy and seemed to grow heavier with each tread of the stairs. Judgement had already been passed on the dog's eventual size. Most who had seen him had commented.

'Look at the size of his paws. Going to be a big dog when he's fully grown.' Samuel and his parents knew otherwise. The breeder had deemed Ben to be a 'failure to thrive' dog that would never amount to much. *It depends what you want him to amount to*, Samuel had thought at the time.

His parents were of the same opinion. 'A dog is whatever you want it to be' was the consensus of the family and, to that end, Ben would do perfectly. As a companion for Samuel he was ideal. As the protector of a small, partially-sighted, boy roaming the country lanes without an adult to defend him, Ben would be second to none. He would come into his own.

And so it turned out to be. On a Sunday morning, when dew lay on the grass and the sun was climbing in the sky, Samuel and Ben would escape into the woodland bordering one side of the house and beyond.

Padding along country lanes to the little church that sat a mile away, Samuel and Ben met few people. On each occasion that they did Ben would lower his head and remain steadfastly between any stranger that came towards them and his charge, Samuel, emitting a low growl from the depths of his chest. He maintained his position until the perceived threat had passed and he and Samuel could resume their walk. So far no-one had challenged them. They knew better than to try to come between a boy and his dog.

The church was their final destination. Not really the church, more the entrance. A wooden roof, perched above a turnstile of sorts, allowed people to enter the churchyard one at a time. Samuel had no wish to enter the church or indeed the churchyard.

He just liked to look at the beautifully constructed entrance known as a Lych Gate. Once done the two turned on their heels and retraced their journey home where a cooked Sunday lunch waited for them.

****

Samuel was crouched between the pages of the book. Desperate to know more of the characters in the story he gingerly leant forwards and turned the page. His fingers were curled round the edge of the smooth, ivory paper as he pulled it towards him. But before he could see what lay on the next page other fingers touched his, another hand met his own.

With a gasp of alarm he released his hold on the page and it slipped from his fingers reluctantly, closing and trapping the story on the other side. The fingers that had met his own were also withdrawn in haste and with not a little grumbling.

'Only wanted to touch his hand. No harm meant,' the little voice murmured reproachfully.

'You were too impatient, Letitia. He is new to the world of books. He does not understand the rules,' reprimanded a stern voice that did not intend to be unkind.

'Only wanted to touch his hand, father,' Letitia repeated soulfully, her voice full of dismay and longing.

'Give him time. He'll be back. He won't be able to resist the lure of the story, the pull of the unknown. Just wait and see.' A feathery-haired woman patted her daughter's shoulders with a reassuring hand.

'Just wait and see...' Letitia echoed, hopeful that indeed this was true and that her mother's prophecy would take place.

During this little family dispute Samuel had not left the book. Although initially alarmed he had stayed put, resting silently within the pages. He had heard every word and was captivated and curious. It seemed as if the voices were coming from the next page, drifting, lilting tongues that stirred his senses. But the hour was late and it had been a long day. Samuel edged further towards the spine of the book and stretched out fully. In no time at all he was asleep.

Chapter 4

Samuel disappears

The winds blew in from the south. They chased the crisp, dried leaves along the stone wall that stood proud and determined against the weather and adversity. The wall was built long before the house and was thought by the villagers to be testament to the many years that the farmer who had owned it worked the land in days gone by.

Back in the early 1800s a man named John Wilkinson had built the wall with the intention of developing it into a barn. Lack of money had resulted in the solitary wall which, if nothing else, had served as a wind break to the rows of vegetables that were sown each year in the land behind it.

In the 1930s, between the two great wars, someone had thought fit to erect a house in the land behind the wall, hoping that the 15 feet high stone erection would protect the house from the worst vagaries of the weather. And so it did, mostly. Except for today when the wind blew from the south. Today the wall served little purpose other than to ruin the line of sight from the window of the house to the open stretches of moorland.

'It's so windy today we could have made good use of a windmill,' Samuel's father muttered under his breath.

'What was that dear?' his wife asked, not really listening for an answer.

'Just complaining about the winds. I'm sure it will calm down soon.'

'I'm sure it will,' his wife agreed, turning her attention fully to the socks she was knitting for her husband. Using three needles, she was knitting in the round. This was a technique that she favoured as the socks were rendered seamless for the most part. More comfortable for the wearer and slower to wear out. A tried and tested method that had never failed.

Meanwhile Samuel slept within the book. He felt comforted within the pages, held and supported during his night's sleep. He normally woke without need of a reminder, as if his body clock alerted him to the fact that the day was upon him and he needed to be up. Today his body clock had let him down. His mother's voice percolated from downstairs unheeded.

'Time to be up Samuel. Your porridge is on the table.' No footsteps were heard on the stairs. No response to the call. His mother, slightly irked by the lack of movement from above, took the unusual step of climbing the stairs to summon Samuel. As she reached the stair before the top, it creaked loudly, in sympathy with the beams of the old house. At the same time it sent out a message that someone was about to walk along the landing.

Samuel was forced to make a difficult decision. Finding himself with one leg out of the book he realised that there was not enough time for him to extricate the rest of his body from the book and appear in his bedroom looking relaxed and unperturbed. The dilemma had but one solution. He quickly withdrew the offending leg back into the book and remained motionless and silent.

Samuel's mother entered his room and saw the empty bed. She glanced quickly round the room, checked the wardrobe in case her son was playing a practical joke then, her anxiety growing by the minute, flew down the stairs calling Samuel's name. His father joined in the search. They looked in all the other rooms in the house and the garden shed. Nothing.

During the ensuing frenzy of activity Samuel quickly left the book, ran to the bathroom and started to wash his face and brush his teeth. At the very moment that his mother appeared at the top of the stairs he appeared from the bathroom looking nonchalant and unabashed.

'Where were you? Five minutes ago. Where were you?' His mother demanded. 'You weren't in your room. I checked. Your father and I have searched the house and garden looking for you. Well?' Standing with her hands on her hips, and apron tied round her waist, Samuel's mother managed to look quite fearsome, though throughout it all he knew that fear had prompted her reaction. Samuel knew better than to lie. He made a poor liar and would be found out the minute he opened his mouth. Better to tell the truth, or a semblance of the truth at any rate.

'I was reading. I had my head in a book,' he offered. 'Sorry.' He hung his head and tried to look ashamed and apologetic. It worked.

'Well wherever you were, next time pay attention when I call you for your breakfast. Your porridge will be cold now but you'll have to eat it as it is. No time to heat it up as you're already late for school.' Samuel nodded and made his way to the breakfast table where a bowl of cold porridge waited for him.

****

There was a new fad at school. Marbles. Amongst the boys and girls alike there was a frantic desire to collect as many as they could. They came in all shapes and sizes. Glass balls that held all the mysteries of the universe. Slips and crescents of colour deep within them that changed with the light. If you held them up and turned them round, the encapsulated colours seemed to have a life of their own and to move independently of the marble held firmly between the fingers.

Marbles were the masters of optical illusion and it seemed to the children that they possessed magical qualities. With small bodies stretched out on the ground, and a look of the utmost concentration on their little faces, the children rolled the marbles in turn, all vying for position. Once rolled, some marbles seemed to be about to stop and then speeded up with renewed energy.

To the children these marbles appeared to have hidden qualities that enabled them to move of their own accord. How else would they carry on rolling once the momentum that had first propelled them had begun to decrease? They all knew it was impossible but still some, extra special, marbles would roll far beyond their anticipated finishing position. These particular marbles were treasured beyond all else and certainly beyond reason.

Some of the 'Ollies', the popular name for marbles in the 1950s, were swapped in the hope that the exchange would prove beneficial to those involved. How this could happen was uncertain but bartering occurred nevertheless.

****

Meanwhile, back in the book, Letitia was tired of waiting. She had little patience at the best of times, a trait that her parents had noticed when she was tiny and still unable to talk. Standing inside her playpen she had demanded a particular toy by dancing up and down, raising her arms and making noises signifying her frustration. Keen not to encourage such behaviour, her parents had ignored all such requests and turned away. Only when she had calmed down would she be presented with the object of her desire.

So Letitia held her tongue and bit back the feelings of irritation that the boy had not been back to visit her. Unbeknown to her, Samuel had visited the book several times since their unwitting encounter; he had not, however, ventured as far as the pages that contained Letitia and her family. She vowed to listen out carefully for the whisper that might tell her when Samuel came again to the land of make believe that dwelled within the book.

Chapter 5

All in the imagination

'Out of sight, out of mind.' The well-known proverb is still heard to this day. For Samuel though, nothing could be further from the truth. Even when he was not inside the book, he was mentally there. For most of his waking hours he would be mentally scanning the pages trying to remember which characters lay on which page. He also had a burning desire to meet once more with the character that had dared to meet his fingertips with theirs at the edge of a page.

At the point where the story was about to expand for Samuel, there was a meeting of hands. The page that lay beyond was still unknown to him. For all he knew there could be a page of writing awaiting him, or a glossy plate that would transfix him with colour and splendour or, the worst scenario, nothing at all. One of those blank pages that seemed to appear within a book for no apparent reason than to indicate a change in story title or to serve as an artificial break within the book.

For Samuel these blank pages had no function at all other than to waste what, to him, was a perfectly good piece of blank paper. Paper that cried out to be written on. One day Samuel would take pen in hand and create his own story, his own characters, his own world of make believe.

Samuel often lived in a world apart. A world of dragons, magic, faeries and unexpected happenings. As early as he could remember he had existed in two worlds. The real one where he went to school, did homework and played games with his friends, and another where all sorts of fantastic creatures graced the air, moved with him as he moved, listened as he read his stories. As a result Samuel was never really alone. His magical friends accompanied him everywhere. It was in his world of make believe that the characters of his imaginings came to the fore and took on a life of their own.

Until he had learned to read, at the age of four, Samuel thought that the characters were all around him in the air. Only when he reached into the world of books did he discover that some of them lay on the written pages within books. As he began to understand the text, the story book people came alive and seemed to talk to him from the page. They appeared to look directly at him and beckon him into the story. Reading books became his favourite past time. Recently, though, events had taken an amazing turn.

It was one evening when he lay tired within the book, between pages one and two as usual, waiting for sleep to come to him. He had in his pyjama pocket some crayons. He idly removed a blue crayon, his favourite colour of the moment, and started to draw on the blank page that currently served as a mattress of sorts. He drew the outline of a bird, a tiny bird that was poised in mid-air in front of a flower. The flower seemed to materialise without Samuel quite being aware that he had drawn it.

As he slowly lifted the crayon from the page, something magical happened. The bird began to move. Its wings, flickering at an incredible speed, appeared to be almost still, such was its ability to hover and remain in one place. Almost static, it gathered nectar from the flower, using a beak that had evolved through millennia for this precise purpose. The Humming bird collected its fill and, without a momentary glance in Samuel's direction, flew away.

All that remained on the page was a flower, isolated in all its splendour against the ivory page that Samuel lay upon. He looked everywhere, eyes darting this way and that, but then the truth stared him in the face. The bird had gone. It was lost to him. As it dawned on him that he had created a bird in a drawing, that had then become invested with life and had risen from the page, Samuel was overwhelmed. He now found it impossible to sleep. He began to draw again, this time inanimate objects that remained on the page. As he reached the last space at the bottom of the ivory sheet of paper he felt for the corner and turned over to a new page. As with most blank pages in a book, both sides were empty.

Samuel was confused as to why anyone would, through choice, leave a page blank within a book. A page that could be filled with wisdom, intrigue, mystery, excitement and possibilities, was rendered inert and useless for no apparent reason. A testament to a gap in the imagination unfilled by inspired thoughts. Almost as if the author of the book had been halted in their tracks by writer's block and had left a page blank, just in case they needed to come back to it at a later date. Another time when imagination had again taken hold of their thoughts and allowed them to once more commit pen to paper. To let the words unfold in front of them, with ease and with a hint of promise for a story that would ripen to the full.

Samuel had filled half of the other side of the blank page before sleep started to overwhelm him. Much as he loved the comfort that the book brought him, tonight he longed for the extra protection and security of an eiderdown, something soft that he could pull over his shoulders and hide his face beneath. As he thought this he heard a rustle below him. Looking towards his feet he saw ripples in the page, ivory threads that seemed to be weaving their way towards him.

The gliding of the threads backwards and forwards, as if driven by an invisible hand wielding a shuttle, fascinated Samuel, mesmerising him to the point where he couldn't take his eyes away from the woven blanket that reached ever higher over his body. In one moment of alarm it crossed his mind that perhaps the weaving would not stop and would cover him completely from his toes to the top of his head, encapsulating him totally within the book.

He need not have worried. His fears were not realised. The weaving continued until the equivalent of an entire page had been produced. An entire page of soft, woven, ivory material that lay on top of him with just enough left over to roll back, just as the sheet lay back over the top of the eiderdown in the bed in his room. The bed that was currently unoccupied because, as always, Samuel was asleep – inside the book.

Chapter 6

The imaginary friend

Samuel had been a very loveable baby. The kind of child that would stop everyone in their tracks when they saw him in his pram. It used to take his mother ages to get to the shops. A mere five minute walk would often extend to twenty minutes or more. Mostly, Samuel's mother did not mind. She loved the attention that Samuel received from strangers and neighbours alike.

'He is so amiable,' someone said to his mother one day. 'As if nothing bothers him.' In actual fact quite a lot bothered Samuel. His smiling features belied an inner turmoil. As he did not start to speak until he was two years old it was often, wrongly, assumed that he did not understand what was going on in his surroundings. Not so. Samuel was a highly intelligent, perceptive child and, while his vision was impaired, there was nothing whatsoever wrong with his hearing. Also, what he was not able to discover using his sight he was often able to assess using the power of touch. His fingers would reach out to touch everything within striking distance as he sought to learn more about the object of his fascination.

From the moment that words began to spill from his mouth, he never looked back. His mother seized the chance to teach him how to read. As if she had held a deep-seated fear that her son might never start to speak, she appeared to want to make up for lost time. Samuel absorbed new words 'like blotting paper' his father would fondly tell any relatives or friends who were unfortunate enough to find themselves on the receiving end of hearing about Samuel's prowess which, if his father were to be believed, touched on genius.

Yes, Samuel's early years were not ordinary. While he appeared slightly withdrawn and less sociable than other children of a similar age, he was a friendly little chap. He was often unable to make out facial expressions of people and, as a result, did not always respond in the expected and socially acceptable manner. As such he was deemed to be 'withdrawn' and 'not forthcoming'. This sad state of affairs had the effect of causing him to withdraw even more into himself and, being someone who liked contact with others, when he felt like it, he took matters into his own hands. He, intentionally or otherwise – who knows? – invented an imaginary friend.

****

Samuel was perched on the window seat in his parents' front room. He was thinking long and hard. Sometimes, when he really wanted to be hidden from view, he would hide himself away inside the window seat. Four of the six panels that formed the seat round the entire length of the bay window could be lifted up. He was still small enough to be able to lower himself in, feet first. Then, in a crouched position, he was able to edge along to another part of the wooden 'tunnel'.

Today, though, he was too absorbed, too pre-occupied, to attempt to conceal himself. The events of the previous evening had taken over his thoughts completely. He could hardly believe what he had witnessed. A bird that he had drawn on a blank page inside his book of make believe had taken on a life of its own and flown off the page. Before his very eyes it had vanished, although Samuel had a sneaking suspicion that it had not gone far and that it might still be somewhere inside the book. Time would tell if he would see it again. Flowers that he had drawn were still rooted on the page and appeared to waft slightly as if a breeze had invited itself into the book, to rustle the pages and create a little disturbance.

Samuel pressed his hands to his temple. Unnoticed by her son, his mother had entered the room and asked if he had a headache. The question had caused him to jolt in alarm. He had thought himself alone and was shaken to the core, shocked by the sudden intrusion into his thoughts. Once he'd remembered where he was, and had realised that there was a question that needed answering, Samuel reassured his mother that he was 'just concentrating'.

He was trying desperately to remember how his imaginary friend had looked, as it was some time since he had communicated with him. Not years exactly, rather months. But months, when you are only eight, can seem like a lifetime. His little friend had been called Peter and had the distinct advantage of being there whenever Samuel felt like he needed some company, and of disappearing whenever he longed to be alone. He was, in every respect, the perfect friend.

Suddenly, Samuel could see a perfect likeness in his mind's eye. Dark, curly hair that touched his collar, navy trousers with boots that laced up to the ankle. A brow that knitted whenever Peter was concentrating on something. A soft voice that he would only raise when he became enthusiastic about something, a V-necked jumper, hand-knitted in maroon wool with an Icelandic pattern round the shoulders. He looked a little odd but, as Samuel had dreamed him up, that was only to be expected. Samuel had a plan and tonight he would carry it out. Tonight he would draw Peter on a blank page in the book. He would try to bring Peter to life properly.

Chapter 7

The creation of Peter

By the time shadows fell Samuel was already inside the book. His mother marvelled that she never had to tell him to go to bed. He took himself there without being asked and with no word of a prompt. Ensconced in his room Samuel ploughed through a few pages of the book before he came to the blank page that he had been drawing on the night before. His heart sank. He had totally forgotten how much of the page he had already used. As what he had drawn was now a permanent fixture on the page it could not be removed. The efforts of an eraser would be fruitless.

However, Samuel was not someone to give up at the first hurdle. He put pen to paper and began to draw. In the three inches of blank paper at the bottom of the page he began to draw with a charcoal pencil, first Peter's hair, framing his face, then his shirt collar, checked material very carefully detailed. Next, the maroon jumper which tucked into his trousers with a leather belt holding everything together. Finally, Peter's boots were traced in outline and the laces pulled together and tied.

It was at this point that Samuel realised that the blank page should have run out ages ago. He raised himself away from the page and looked down. He saw that he had moved on to a new blank page. The book had created a new page for him to draw on. Not only was Samuel able to create characters, such as the Humming bird that came to life, but he was extending the book in the process. He looked down at Peter who promptly smiled at him, and raised a hand as if in request to be lifted up. Samuel pulled his friend towards him and hugged him.

'You're alive,' he managed to stutter through his tears.

'Well of course I'm alive. I'm a person just like you, only before you only saw what you imagined me to be, a faint echo of who I am. Now you see the real me.'

****

Samuel and Peter were running. They ran for the sheer love of it. They ran as if their lives depended on it. Their feet barely touched the surface as they skimmed the pages of the book. Before they knew it they had reached page 24. They had barely glanced at the words printed beneath them as they flew by, so had no idea whereabouts in the story they had ended up.

The going had started to get a little difficult in places. Up until now they had moved easily, through woodland, along a path lined with primroses, where birds chattered and squirrels leapt along branches. Deep in the wood they had glimpsed bluebells. Now they were forced to slow down.

'Can you remember anything of the story in the book?' Samuel asked Peter. Peter shook his head.

'Me neither,' Samuel spoke more out of a sense of loss than anything else.

'Do you know where we are?' asked Peter.

'No, I've no idea,' Samuel was now beginning to grow anxious. What if they couldn't find their way back? In theory it should be straight forward. They need only follow the page numbers in reverse order. Ever decreasing numbers would mean that they were nearing the front of the book. Samuel had only ever entered the book from the front and it was there that they must make for.

With a glance to the skies he noticed, with some trepidation, that heavy clouds were brooding overhead and the sky was beginning to darken. As they were still on page 24, and had not yet begun to move back to the beginning of the book, he was not quite sure how they would do this. He had always thought that, once words were printed on a page, the story was fixed there forever, unchangeable, offered up for all eternity as something that could not be broken or altered.

Samuel started to wonder if this might not actually be the case; that the story might be changed. Depending on who or what looked on its pages, and engaged with the characters, maybe the story could indeed be altered. Then the incident with the fingers in the book leapt into his mind. Someone had touched his fingers with theirs. Round the edge of a page, that he had been turning, someone else's hand had met his. Someone else dwelled within the book. He voiced his concerns to Peter.

'We must look for them,' Peter said. 'We must search for the person who lives beyond the next page.' Then, in a statement that showed that Samuel was indeed wise beyond his years and demonstrated a deep, inner knowing, he replied.

'Yes, but maybe they live always just beyond the next page.' Peter looked quickly at his friend, rather unnerved by his quiet outburst. It seemed that there was more to living in a book than either of them had first thought.

'We must find the page with the church on it. The church that has a clock on its spire,' Samuel's voice had taken on an urgent note. 'I have to be up in time for breakfast or my mother will come looking for me. The other day I didn't quite make it out of the book in time and a disaster nearly befell me!' Samuel paused when he realised what he'd said and then slowly reformed his words. 'I meant when a disaster nearly happened.'

Peter couldn't see the difference between the two sentences but Samuel was painfully aware that since he had taken to visiting the book, and spending whole nights between its pages, his speech had begun to alter. Small things at first. Barely noticeable nuances. But these small hiccups of language had grown to the point where Samuel felt he almost needed to think twice before he opened his mouth. When he sat and read the book, with it open in front of him, he saw that the language used had a slightly archaic style to it, a rather old-fashioned turn of phrase. One evening he had asked his father where the book had come from.

'Which book is that then?' His father was happy to help as always.

'The old leather one with the picture on the front.' Samuel took his father to his room and pointed at the book on the table beside his bed. He could have carried the book downstairs to the living room but he had no wish to move it from its usual place.

'Well, you know, I don't ever remember buying this book,' his father passed his hand over the gilt-edged cover and spine. 'It reminds me of the kind of book that you find in the back of very old book shops. I don't recognise the title or the author either for that matter. Josef Ungermach...' he mused. 'Unusual name. Sounds German, or Swiss, possibly. Maybe it came with the house. Where did you find it?'

'It just seemed to be there on my bedside table one morning when I woke up, and it's been there ever since,' Samuel finished. Since this brief discussion about the book Samuel had not drawn his parents' attention to it. He forced his mind back to the present. They concentrated on the job in hand and finally found themselves at the beginning of the book.

'I must be off. See you tonight.' And with that Samuel unfolded himself from the leaves of the book, landing softly on the bed. Peter was now left to his own devices and, as the whole day lay before him, he decided to explore the book and see where his adventures took him. He would start on page one.

Chapter 8

In search of Peter

It was parents' evening at Samuel's school and he was slightly apprehensive. He sat on a chair, wedged between his parents. The chair was positioned, it almost appeared, so that escape was not possible.

His eyes darted anxiously to the face of the first teacher on the list, Mr Fairbanks. As the class teacher he was responsible for teaching most of the subjects, but there was also a teacher in charge of pastoral care and another, Emma Darling, whose purpose was to help the children develop their creative abilities.

Mr Fairbanks smiled amiably at Samuel and showered him with praise noting only that 'he does tend to wander off into his imagination at times – but if you can't do that when you're eight then when can you do it?' and, in so doing, answered his own question.

Mrs Walters, in charge of pastoral care, seemed rather more concerned with 'Samuel's ability to drift off into his own world at a moment's notice.' She pointed out that this was 'a little worrying as he is missing parts of his lesson.'

Samuel's parents nodded sagely and adopted a concerned look that mirrored that of Mrs Walters. In their hearts, though, they were not remotely concerned about 'Samuel drifting off'.

'He's bright enough. He'll catch up,' his mother whispered to his father when the teacher and their small son were out of earshot. The third and last of the teachers was Emma Darling, Samuel's favourite teacher, who taught music. She beamed at him as the group of three approached her table.

'Samuel is one of my most enthusiastic and able pupils,' she told his parents. No-one can learn, carry and hold a tune quite like Samuel. He absolutely excels at this. He only has to hear a tune played through once and it is there in his head. Two weeks later I can ask him to hum it and he does, with no problem. Note perfect. He can read the music if he needs to. As you know, all our sheet music is printed with larger print than usual and is also readable in braille format.' Then, turning to Samuel: 'But you manage fine don't you Samuel?' He nodded, glowing with the praise heaped upon him. 'What would you say is your favourite instrument do you think?' she asked. Samuel thought for a moment.

'Probably the melodeon,' he said. 'I can run my fingers up and down the keys easily without having to look at them. It's easier than playing the guitar, when you have to keep finding the right fret.'

He stopped. The three adults were looking at him, rather awe struck.

'I think that's very well put,' Mrs Lang was the first to break the silence. Her simple statement failed to voice what all of them were thinking, namely that Samuel had never spoken so eloquently or, indeed, for that long, ever.

'He really enjoys reading books too,' Samuel's mother was keen to keep the conversation rolling. 'One book in particular actually. A rather ancient, leather-bound book that he keeps beside his bed. He's never out of it. Whenever I can't find him I can be sure that he's inside the book.' Little did she realise how true her words were!

****

When Samuel crept between the pages of the book that evening Peter was nowhere to be seen. There was neither hide nor hair of him. Samuel made a mental note to get up early in the morning to search for his friend before leaving for school. He tried to remember how many pages were in the book, how many printed ones and how many blank ones, and he started to count them in his head. His mouth made the shape of 'fourteen' and then he fell into a sound sleep. As he lay there, covered by the ivory threads of woven blanket, characters from the book emerged from the shadows to gaze upon him.

'He isn't very big for a human is he?' said one.

'Well, he's still growing. Don't forget that,' another stood up for him. Tiny faeries hovered above him, lighting the shadows with a touch of their wands.

'We will take care of him while he sleeps. Have no fear.' They spoke in unison to the gathered throng.

'Why does he have to come into the book in the first place? Why doesn't he just read it like anyone else would?' asked a rather grumpy-looking man who was leaning heavily on a stick for support.

'He is looking for comfort in the words on the pages. He loves the feeling that they give him. Warm and safe. That's how they make him feel.'

'And how would you know that?' asked the grumpy old man.

'Because I am his friend.' Peter stood up to be counted. As always, he was not one to keep his head low and avoid stating his purpose. He was not afraid to speak the truth. Peter was a person of sound mind and conscience.

'You're his friend?' a timid voice murmured from the background.

'Yes. Who are you? Please show yourself,' Peter asked, and Letitia stepped out of the shadows.

'Our fingers met once but that was a long time ago.' Her voice faded and sounded wistful. 'Would you like to meet Samuel – properly?' suggested Peter.

'Oh yes please,' Letitia breathed out words that held the promise and expectation of things to come.

'Then I will arrange it,' promised Peter.

'How can Samuel be your friend when you live in the book and he lives in the real world?' asked a tin soldier whose uniform had seen better days.

'He drew me and I came to life. I was his imaginary friend when he was a small child and he drew a likeness of me so here I am.' The others gasped and looked incredulous.

'Can he draw anything and make it come to life?' asked a small girl wearing a pinafore dress and carrying a wooden bucket.

'Yes, I think so. He drew a humming bird the other day and it flew off the page and disappeared somewhere else in the book,' Peter told them.

'That would explain the exotic bird that landed on some flowers in my garden the other day. It seemed to be taking something from the centre of the flowers.'

'Yes, that would have been the Humming bird taking nectar,' confirmed Peter.

'Does Samuel know that we are all alive and are real characters within the book?' asked Letitia's father, who had been listening to the conversation. 'Although I think he might suspect after his fingers touched Letitia's,' he continued.

'Could he make some other things come alive by drawing them?' asked a rather upright figure wearing garden overalls.

'I'm sure he could,' said Peter. 'I will ask him in the morning and see what he says.' This seemed to satisfy the throng and they began to disperse and wend their way back to their particular story within the book. All except one, who lagged behind.

'Please Peter. Please can I be first to speak with Samuel?' she pleaded.

'I will try to arrange it,' Peter promised.

****

When morning came all was quiet in the book. The figures who had descended onto the page where Samuel lay sleeping were all busy living their own lives, in their own stories. Only the clock was keeping pace with events, measuring time and lending structure to the lives of those who dwelled within the make-believe book.

Samuel stretched and felt for the next page of the book. There lay the clock, a two-dimensional time-keeper that appeared perfectly flat on the page but nevertheless had a second, a minute and an hour hand that were perfectly reliable. He knew this as he regularly checked this clock against the clock in his bedroom. They were always identical. Samuel liked things to be reliable.

To allow for those mornings when he awoke, and it was still dark, he had used a pin to raise dots on the paper clock in the book. He read it as he would read braille. The clock never let him down. Right now the clock's hands stood at five minutes to seven. This left only five minutes for Samuel to search for Peter.

He hastily rose, shrugging off the ivory-threaded, self-woven blanket. He used his sensitive finger tips, as well as his eyes, to look for his friend. On the pages where the light was reduced, and where the illustration showed a scene at night time, he found that touch was most definitely a better tool to use when searching.

He whispered 'Peter, are you there?' The whispered breath carried on through the book, unhindered by words or blank pages. It didn't fade until it had reached the ears of the one for whom it was intended. Peter stirred in his sleep to find Letitia by his side patting his arm gently.

'That's Samuel calling isn't it? He wants you to go to him. Can I come too?' she asked timidly but with a sense of urgency in her voice. Peter rallied to the situation and immediately pulled on his coat, not knowing how the weather would turn out once he had left the cosy warmth of his bed in the little house in the square. The little house that stood with several others and formed the community known as 'Safe Haven Village'.

'Let us go,' Peter took Letitia's hand and they left the little house just as the sun appeared over the horizon. The pair scrambled over the hillside, turned pages, ran as fast as their legs would carry them. But it was not fast enough. When they reached the page where Samuel had been sleeping, all that remained was a light imprint on the page to show that he had been there. But Samuel had gone.

Chapter 9

The castle

School lessons would not happen today. It was the day of the school trip. Once a year, just before the Easter holidays, class three, Samuel's class, would make the journey to the castle in the woods. Most schools chose the seaside, but not Samuel's. Being a school for partially-sighted children, the teachers were more imaginative when it came to deciding what would thrill the children most on a day out.

It was no ordinary castle, as Samuel would soon discover, although it appeared normal with stone turrets and a small drawbridge over a moat. Once all the children, and the teachers accompanying them, had entered the castle, the drawbridge was pulled up. No-one could now enter or leave the castle.

Safety was paramount and the temporary sealing off from the outside world meant that the children could run about to their heart's content, unhindered by well-meaning calls to 'watch your step' and 'mind how you go'. It was freedom of the ultimate kind and Samuel loved it.

Samuel was not without friends. One in particular, Jocelyn, drew him to her, day in and day out. Jocelyn lived in a land of make believe and Samuel was fascinated by her. 'Tell me a story,' he would ask. 'Tell me the one with faeries in it.' And Jocelyn would oblige. Today, though, Samuel longed for Peter's company. Peter, however, was sadly confined to the book that sat on Samuel's bedside table.

Samuel wandered off on his own through the castle and found himself in a long corridor. Dimly lit by lights in little alcoves, the corridor seemed to be rather imposing and scary. Also, the door at the end of the corridor that Samuel was making for, didn't seem to be getting any nearer. In fact, the faster he walked, the further away it seemed.

Not possible he thought. He felt as if he was walking up an escalator that was moving downwards. No matter how fast he ran upwards, the escalator would still take him down.

Then, suddenly, the door was directly in front of him. One minute it had lain far ahead of him at the end of a long corridor and now it was so close he could touch it. He reached out for the door knob and turned it. Nothing happened. *It must be locked* he thought. He tried it again and this time the door swung open to reveal a small room. This was not just any room. It was his bedroom at home.

Samuel thought he must be dreaming. He closed the door and opened it again. The room looked the same. There was his bed with a table beside it and a little rug on the floor. Even the curtains looked identical.

Then it dawned on Samuel. There was one crucial difference between this room and his bedroom back at home. The book was missing. The bedside table was bare. He breathed a sigh of relief. The book would be safe at home. There was no need to worry. He took another look round the room, turned towards the door and was about to close it when he heard a little voice.

'Please help me. I'm lost. I fell out of the book.' Samuel looked about the room for the origin of the voice. There, standing beside the skirting board, was a very small girl, barely three inches tall.

'I know you Samuel,' she said, looking directly at him. 'You visit the book where I live. You sleep in our book.' Samuel racked his brains, then an illustration from the book swam in front of his field of vision. This was a child that belonged to one of the families in the book. She could normally be found on page 12, holding hands with her little brother as they ran up a hillside.

'What is your name?' asked Samuel, cautiously curious.

'Hannah. My name is Hannah.' The little figure looked so anxious and worried that Samuel's heart went out to her.

'I know you too,' he said. 'I recognise you from page 1 of the book. How did you manage to fall out of it?'

'Dick, my brother, and I were running across the page and I tripped and fell off the edge of the page and out of the book.'

'How on earth did you end up here, in a room that looks like my bedroom, but isn't, inside a castle?'

'I really don't know,' Hannah replied. 'Perhaps this is a magical castle and it has brought you to me so you can help me back into the book?' Samuel couldn't see how this was remotely possible but was keen to help the little lost character from his precious book.

'Come to me. Climb onto my hand. I will put you in my coat pocket and carry you safely back to my house. Then you can come back into the book with me when I go to sleep at night. Or we can see if it's possible for you to go back in the book as soon as we get back to my house.' Hannah looked greatly relieved at this idea and climbed onto Samuel's hand. Once tucked away in his pocket she felt safe and secure and fell into a deep sleep.

Samuel now had a real challenge. He had to spend the rest of the day roaming the castle with his school friends, knowing all the time that he was carrying a precious cargo in his coat pocket. He left the room and found his friends in time for lunch. They sat around a large table eating the food that they had brought with them. It was warm inside the castle as a fire was burning brightly at one end of the room. Samuel began to grow hot under the collar. He started to become hotter and hotter until his cheeks were flushed scarlet. One of the teachers, Mr Fairbanks, was growing concerned about Samuel's wellbeing.

'Are you alright Samuel? You look very warm. Wouldn't you like to take off your coat?' But taking off his coat was the last thing that Samuel was prepared to do. He was terrified that if he lost sight of his coat, for even a second, or put it down on a chair, that someone would sit on it and, in the process, squash little Hannah. Hannah, who was completely unaware of Samuel's dilemma as she was fast asleep in his pocket, dreaming dreams of being home, racing up the hillside with her brother Dick, in the book.

The day seemed to last forever but, finally, they were on the journey home. Samuel was exhausted with worry but his face became a picture of happiness when his father picked him up from school.

'Did you enjoy your trip to the castle,' he asked his son.

'Yes, it was quite good,' Samuel replied, secretly relieved beyond belief that he was finally heading back to his home and the book.

'I'm just going to read my book before tea,' he shouted down to his parents as he headed up the stairs to his room. Hurriedly closing the door he gently lifted sleeping Hannah from the pocket of his coat.

'Where are we?' she asked, rubbing her eyes sleepily.

'We're back in my real bedroom. Now you can go back into the book.' Samuel thought about how he entered the book. He would turn to the first page, lay his cheek upon it and then find that his whole body was suddenly on the page. Hopefully, the same method would work for Hannah.

'Here Hannah. I have opened the book at page 12.' As he spoke the words he looked at the illustration on the page. Hannah was not in it. Even though he knew, in his heart, that this would be the case, he was still shocked to see her missing from the picture, and he thought he could detect sadness in the expression on her brother's face. Hannah's brother, who he now knew to be called Dick, was halfway up a hillside without his sister beside him.

'Just lie down on the page and I will close the book gently. You should then become part of the picture again.'

'I do hope so.' Hannah did not look convinced but did as Samuel suggested all the same. The minute her body was on the page Samuel carefully closed the book, frightened in case he might injure her. He need not have worried. He counted to ten then opened the book again at page 12. There was Hannah, her face beaming out from the page with an equally happy brother standing beside her. Holding hands they appeared to be frozen in time, half-way up a hillside.

Chapter 10

A misunderstanding

Many days had elapsed since Samuel and Peter had last met in the book. Peter longed to see his little friend and hoped that he hadn't said anything to upset him; something that would have made Samuel stay away from him.

He need not have worried. Samuel had indeed been in the book every night. On the stroke of ten o'clock his head would rest on the first page as the book drew him into itself, covering him with the ivory-threaded blanket for warmth, comfort and protection.

Samuel had been very busy lately. He had after-school club some days, football practice on others, and helped his mother to clean out the chickens on the allotment every night.

Samuel certainly led a very full life. A life that was satisfying and filled him with content. Through it all, though, he harboured a sense of regret. Regret that he did not have more time to spend meeting the characters in the book and finding out how they lived their lives.

The summer holidays were just around the corner, then Samuel would have the time he so craved. Then he would be able to investigate the stories that the book held within it, follow the tales as they unwound, page by page. He had given some thought to how he might prevent himself from getting lost within the book. He would loop a piece of cotton over the clasp on the front of the book. Attached round his wrist, the cotton would follow his movements as he trailed off through the book. To get back to the beginning he need only follow the cotton. It would be easy.

That night Samuel went to bed early. Anxious to spend some time travelling through the stories, before sleep overcame him, he crept into the book just before nine o'clock. If his parents were surprised at his eagerness to go to bed early they didn't show it.

He wished he knew how to step into the book at any page he chose, rather than having to start at the beginning and work his way through it. It was not that he minded pushing his way through the stories, it was more that the first few were all very familiar to him and he wanted to visit new stories, have new experiences. Above all he wanted to find Peter. And Letitia wanted to find Samuel.

Samuel sprinted across page 12 to see that both Hannah and Dick were not in the illustration and must be off somewhere else in the book, having fun. He smiled to himself, happy in the knowledge that he had been able to help out little Hannah in her hour of need. He raced over page 15 and bumped into someone coming in the opposite direction.

'Peter!' 'Samuel!' They spoke at the same time, happy to be reunited.

'Samuel, there is someone who wants to meet you. Here is Letitia.' A small fair-haired slip of a girl edged forwards across the page offering her hand to Samuel as she did so. Out of politeness Samuel took the little hand in his and shook it.

'Pleased to meet you Letitia. You must tell me your story.'

'I would be glad to,' Letitia whispered.

'But first I must sleep,' Samuel said. 'I feel very tired tonight. Tomorrow is the first day of the summer holidays so I will be free to listen to stories.' Letitia was more than happy to hear this and promised to return the next day.

Samuel woke slowly. His head ached and his tummy hurt. He felt as if he had walked into a wall and eaten something that disagreed with him – at the same time. He struggled out of the book and made it downstairs, still wearing his pyjamas.

'You look poorly Samuel,' his mother said. 'How do you feel?' she asked, putting her hand to his forehead as she spoke.

'I don't feel very well,' Samuel managed.

'Well, I think you should try to drink something to keep your fluid levels up. Then maybe you should go back to bed and try to sleep. I have to go out but my friend Jean will be dropping in before I leave. She's coming to collect some things to take to the charity shop. I've asked her to keep an eye on you. You won't notice she's here. She'll be busy packing charity shop things and I'll be back soon after.'

Samuel headed back to his room with a piece of toast and marmalade in one hand and a cup of tea in the other. His bed looked inviting but the book won, as always. Having eaten the toast, and drunk the tea, Samuel crept inside the book and fell asleep.

Jean heard the front door close as Samuel's mother came in.

'Thanks for looking after him Jean.'

'It was no problem,' Jean replied. 'I put my head round his door and he seemed to be covered up in his bed so I didn't disturb him. I've got all the books that you said I could have for the charity shop. Thanks very much, by the way.'

'You're welcome,' replied Samuel's mother, anxious for her friend to leave so she could check on Samuel. She ran up the stairs two at a time to see how her little son was feeling. The bed didn't look quite right. A bit rumpled but not quite right. She patted the eiderdown flat and her fears were realised. No-one was in the bed. Granted it was rather dishevelled and, at first glance looked like a small eight-year-old boy might be beneath the bed clothes, but no – the bed was empty. She cast her eyes round the room and they came to rest on the bedside table. It was empty. The book had gone. Thoughts raced through her mind. Someone had taken Samuel and they had also stolen the book. Trying to stay calm Samuel's mother reached for the phone.

'Jean, did you notice anything unusual when you checked on Samuel in his room?'

'Not particularly. His bed looked as if he was in it and I didn't want to disturb him by investigating further. Is there a problem?' Jean enquired, anxious to put her friend's mind at rest.

'I'm not sure. When I checked his room Samuel was not in his bed. Strange also was that his beloved ancient leather tome, with a clasp, that always sits on his bedside table, had gone.'

'Oh no!' Jean was mortified. 'I thought that was one of the books that I was to collect and take to the charity shop.' Samuel's mother became very agitated when she heard this.

'No. It was only meant to be the books on the dining room table, not the one from Samuel's bedroom, that were to go to the charity shop. Where is the book? Do you still have it?'

'I'm afraid not. I dropped them all off at the shop just before it closed this afternoon. I'll go there first thing in the morning. With any luck they won't have sold it and I can bring it straight back to Samuel.'

Samuel. Where could he be? His mother searched the house and garden, but no Samuel. He was nowhere to be found. As dusk fell his parents phoned the police and a search was organised with neighbours from the village offering their help and joining in. Some brought their dogs. Dogs that had proved their worth as tracker dogs and could easily detect Samuel's scent.

If the dogs were to be relied on, a startling conclusion was reached as midnight struck. Samuel had not been stolen from his room. In fact he had not left it all. At some point during the time between his mother leaving the house, and returning, Samuel had vanished within the confines of his room. He was not lost from the house. He was, however, lost to them. And the book was another matter entirely.

Chapter 11

Lost in the woods

Light rays of sun filtered through the sheaves of thin pages where the edges were raised slightly. Samuel's small frame lay within the book between pages one and two as usual. He had spent a restless night tossing and turning, as a fever had taken hold of him, done its worst, and left him drained. As dawn was breaking he woke and was instantly overwhelmed by thirst. He edged towards the bottom of the page and tipped himself carefully out of the book. But it was not his bedroom floor that met with his feet, nor was it the familiar surroundings of his bedroom that met with his gaze.

He took an involuntary step backwards as his brain tried to assess what had happened and where he was. The book was resting on a table, true, but not his bedside table. This was a long, functional dining table crafted from rough wood. It had taken a hammering from years of use and a general lack of care. Copper pans hung from the rafters over a large range at one end of what could only be described as a kitchen. An old collie dog was curled up on a rug in front of the range. The dog opened her eyes slightly and squinted at Samuel, then closed them again. *Not much of a guard dog* thought Samuel, followed by *I know this dog. It's Peggy. She lives on the farm along the lane from my house. How on Earth have I, and the book, ended up here?*

Samuel wasted no time. He grabbed the make-believe book from the table, stuffed it inside his pyjama top then looked for a coat to wear. He couldn't venture outside in pyjamas. Everyone would look at him. It just couldn't happen. Feeling a little like a thief, albeit an unintentional one, he grabbed what looked like a coat used as an overall when milking the cows. It was too big, by far, but was the only thing to hand so would have to do. Then Samuel, book hidden on his person, hot-footed it through the back door and across the fields.

He approached his house with caution, having caught sight of a police car sitting outside. Entering through the front door was not an option. He headed for a door that led to a utility room, and from there to the back stairs leading off the kitchen. He managed to make it undetected to his bedroom. Once there he laid the book on the table beside his bed and climbed into the bed pulling the eiderdown over his head as he did so. He fell asleep almost immediately but was shocked into the world by a loud voice exclaiming:

'He's here. He's in his bed.' His mother's voice.

'Not possible. We've searched the room from top to bottom several times. He was most definitely not in his room. Not anywhere!' His father sounded dumb-founded.

'Samuel, where were you?' His mother's voice, softer now.

'In my bed. But I did go for a walk in the night. I felt drawn to the woods. I was so hot and needed a cool breeze on my head. I had a fever.' His mother felt his head.

'And you still have a fever. You're going nowhere. I'll bring you a cup of tea. Do you feel like any breakfast?'

'Maybe a piece of toast and marmalade?' Samuel asked, feeling greatly relieved that he had thought quickly and come up with a reason why he had been out and about when he should have been in bed. If only dogs could talk Samuel's secret would have been revealed. The sniffer dogs knew for certain that Samuel was not in his bed at all during the night and Peggy, the farm dog, knew exactly where he had been. If only dogs could talk.

****

It was all getting a bit much. Trying to steer a fine line between living his life in the real world and visiting the world that lay within the book was becoming more and more difficult. The only time that Samuel could realistically spend time with the story book characters was at night when he was supposed to be tucked up in his bed asleep. Even if he made excuses, and went to bed early, there was always the chance that one or other of his parents might pop their head round his bedroom door to wish him 'good night, sleep tight, make sure the bugs don't bite'. Samuel hated this expression. For the life of him, he could not understand why anyone would think that it might be a good thing to say to someone who was about to go to sleep and enter the world of dreams. Having his thoughts turned to bugs biting was the last thing he wanted.

No, it was all getting too risky. He really wanted, no - needed, to spend more time in the book. He wanted to become involved in the lives of the characters, to see Letitia again and to spend more time with Peter, his faithful friend.

****

Samuel decided to go for a walk in the woods. This always helped him to think. He wandered over to the neighbouring farm that he had only left the day before in his frantic rush across the fields, book hidden away, fever on his brow. Peggy, as ever, was willing to go with him. He whistled her out of the barn where she was crouched, paying close attention to the playful antics of baby rats. Before she'd had chance to pounce she had responded to Samuel's tuneless whistle and raced out of the barn. She might sleep deeply at night but, for a relatively old dog, she was remarkably agile.

'Let's go to the woods,' Samuel told Peggy as he patted her head. The words were rather unnecessary as the path they followed was always the same. They reached a clearing in the wood and hid away inside the hollow trunk of an ancient oak. Samuel had barely begun to explain the nature of his problem to Peggy when it hit him. A solution to the problem. He must move the book. If he told his parents he was going to be out all day looking for tadpoles in ponds, and generally wandering round in the wood, there would be no problem. With Peggy guarding his every movement it couldn't be simpler.

He wouldn't take his own puppy, Ben, with him just yet. Ben was still too boisterous and very bad at keeping still and quiet. Peggy, on the other hand, could be trusted with his life, as indeed his parents did. Yes, this was the way forward. Disappear into the woods with the book.

The next day, Samuel had his plan in place.

'I'm off Mum,' he shouted over his shoulder as he slipped out of the door, closing it swiftly behind him. Scuffling, whimpering sounds could be heard as Ben, his new puppy, strove to follow him on his wanderings. Samuel loved Ben and felt a tug of guilt as he plunged into the woodland bordering one side of his parents' house. Not a time to take Ben with him, especially considering what he had in mind today. Today was the day he planned to enter the book during broad daylight and away from the secure environment of his bedroom.

Collecting Peggy on the way, from the neighbouring farm, the pair soon reached the edge of the woods. The day before Samuel had caught sight of a large oak tree with a crumbling centre where he thought he might hide away for his adventure in the book. With Peggy lying at the opening to the tree, Samuel laid the book on the ground inside the hollow.

To a passer by the book looked nothing special. But for its ancient appearance, with embossed leather cover and silver clasp, that suggested that some value might be attached to it, the book did not warrant a second look, nor even ask for one. The book was constant in itself. It was content to let others live and let live, provided that they afforded the same respect to it.

Samuel did not yet know it but the book, should it be subject to attack or any disregard for its well-being, was capable of reprisals. It was not a book to be trifled with. To Samuel, at this particular moment, the book appeared quite benign; a treasure trove of characters interwoven into stories. Stories that were there for reading, to venture into and to emerge from as never quite the same person. Engaging with a story, in the fullest sense, meant that it would change a person forever. Give them a new insight into how they functioned in the world. Show them how to live their life to the full and, above all, how their imagination could take them to new heights and create a new aspect to all things. Yes, once having been inside a story, you would indeed live to tell the tale. But it would be a different tale.

The Sun dodged behind a cloud and the temporary shadowing of the hollow in the tree gave Samuel the perfect moment for entering the book. With stealth and utmost swiftness he vanished, leaving only a book and a dog keeping guard.

Samuel moved quickly through the book. He had found that if he did not announce his presence by whistling, or by sending out a whisper, he could travel relatively unnoticed within the book. It was as if, by failing to engage with any of the characters, or the stories themselves, as the stories failed to have any impact on him, so he failed to have any impact on the stories.

He speeded past page 12 with Hannah and Dick halfway up the hillside and thought he noticed a momentary flash of recognition on Hannah's face as she glimpsed him turning the page to enter the story on page 14.

After much scanning Samuel found Peter. His friend was in the square of the little group of houses that made up Safe Haven Village. Even though Peter had been created by Samuel's own hand he had easily found his way in the book. Open arms had reached out and welcomed him into their lives. Smiling faces had offered him a home.

And so it was that Samuel came upon Peter playing a game of hopscotch with Letitia in the square. Chalked marks on the stones. So simple, yet so enticing. Numbers to aim for. Other children stood round and cheered on Letitia as she reached the end of the chalked squares. Then all fell silent as faces turned to look at Samuel. Not out of fear, or alarm, but out of curiosity.

'Samuel! You're here!' Peter was delighted. 'Let me introduce you to my friends. First, Letitia. Actually you have already met. Your fingers touched once across a page.' Letitia smiled shyly and took Samuel's hand. It had never entered Samuel's mind before but, as he stood in the square of Safe Haven Village, with the sun climbing into the sky and a light breeze playing over the tops of the daffodils, he realised that he was the same size as everyone around him. The book had shrunk him.

From the moment Samuel began to enter the book he started to become smaller so that he could fit into one page and sleep comfortably all night. There was one other possibility of course, namely that Samuel did not become smaller in order that he could get inside the book, but rather that the book grew bigger in order to accommodate him. He thought the last possibility to be the least likely of the two scenarios, especially as it would mean everything and everyone in the book growing bigger to meet his size. Still, it was an option to bear in mind for the future. Who knew what the book was capable of?

Samuel was keeping an eye on the clock. He had spent a pleasant afternoon in the company of Peter, Letitia and their friends. They had remained within the square, having felt no need to wander further afield. At the top of the spire that towered majestically above the village church stood a clock. It could be seen from miles around. Word had it that any person that dwelled within the book should be able to see the clock from wherever they happened to be. But in truth this only worked if they managed to scale a hillside to reach higher ground or if they were able to look out of the window of the upper storey of a house. In reality, the clock could only be viewed clearly by those who lived out their lives in Safe Haven Village.

'Do you have school here?' Samuel asked, idly scuffing the ground with his shoes, happily aware that his mother was not there to scold him for mistreating them.

'Yes. We go to school every day except Sunday,' said Letitia. 'But we only have classes between 8.00 am and 12.00 pm then we are free from school for the rest of the day,' she added.

'Free to do what you want?' Samuel gasped in amazement.

'Not always free,' Peter came in. 'When it's time to harvest the crops everyone is expected to lend a hand, no matter how small they are. All the villagers that is.' Samuel could not decide if life in Safe Haven Village was better or worse than his own life. He suspected that neither was indeed better or worse than the other. They were just different. He looked once more towards the clock, then to the heavens.

'It's getting late and the sky is darkening,' he told Peter. 'I should go before the rain comes. With luck I should reach page one before the heavens open.' Farewells were bidden and promises made to meet again soon. In no time at all Samuel was sliding out of the book into the hollowed out trunk of the tree. He looked for Peggy, but she had gone. Panic filled his entire being and he ran as fast as his legs could carry him, heading for home.

Dusk was beginning to fall and with it ominous shadows that thrust themselves in Samuel's path and threatened his resolve. Finger-like projections of inky black that unnerved him and melted the hard outline of the path into a grey blended fuzziness that became ever harder to follow. He could no longer see the path clearly. The fading light made it particularly difficult for Samuel, with his impaired vision, to see where it was taking him. He could no longer make out the edge of the wood and anxiety took hold of him as he became convinced that, instead of leaving the wood, he was moving further and further into it. Just as his heart plunged into despair he heard a bark. Relief shone in his eyes as Peggy bounded up to him, covering his face with kisses, so pleased was she to see him.

'Peggy. You found me!' He was overcome with gratitude and relief. Feeling for her collar he let her lead him out of the dark wood and into the field beyond. Lights from the farmhouse windows flooded the fields with their welcoming amber glow. Peggy, feeling the need in Samuel for further guidance, led him to his parents' door where she slunk away into the gloom. He let himself in.

'Is that you Samuel?' his father shouted from his study. 'We were just beginning to worry. Dusk is well upon us and you weren't home. Then someone said they'd seen Peggy hunting for rats in the far field when we knew she should have been with you. We told ourselves that they must have been mistaken as Peggy would never let you out of her sight.' And indeed Peggy had not let Samuel out of her sight. He had let her out of his sight. From the moment he had entered the book, as far as Peggy was concerned, he was no longer there to warrant protecting. The level of protection Peggy would provide for him obviously far outweighed what she would provide for a book. In Peggy's case the old adage was certainly true: 'out of sight, out of mind'.

Chapter 12

The drought

The residents of Safe Haven Village were having a meeting. The Village Hall was full to the rafters with folk of all ages and sizes crammed into every available space. Every nook and cranny was occupied by a villager craning their neck, eager to catch every word that was being spoken.

The mayor addressed his people. He looked like any other villager, save for the embroidered waistcoat and the black felt hat perched jauntily on his head with a feather adorning it.

'We are gathered here today to discuss a most urgent matter. Most urgent indeed.' He paused to look round the throng and to ensure that they were taking in every word.

'Yes, a very grave matter indeed.' Repeating his words only served to irritate some of the listeners and to cause disquiet amongst the others. One could contain herself no longer.

'What is it mayor? Tell us please.'

'All in good time,' the mayor replied in a calm manner that belied his original statement that the matter was urgent.

'You will all be aware that we have suffered a serious drought this year. January was very dry, February too, and March also saw very little rain. Since then – nothing. We are now in June and our crops are dying. You know that we have tried everything we know to bring down the rain. Rituals well used for centuries have failed to result in a single drop of precious water. Soon, it will not only be the crops that are suffering, it will be us. Our wells will begin to run dry.'

The murmurs of agreement and anxiety played around the hall, like waves on the shore. The mayor had their full attention.

'So, what can be done? Well, I have an idea. I hope you will think it is a good one.' Each and every one of them held their breath in anticipation of the mayor's next words. A pin could have been dropped at that moment and all would have turned and jolted in alarm at the unexpected intrusion of noise into their silent space.

'Most of you know that we have had a visitor in the book. Samuel. Many of you have met him; or if not actually met him, will have heard of him. I propose that we ask Samuel for his help.' He looked round the hall trying to assess the mood of the villagers.

'But he's only eight,' cried one. 'How can a boy of eight help us in our hour of need?'

'Just so,' the mayor replied. 'He is indeed only eight, but Samuel is special. A boy in a million. He is gifted and intelligent and above all he is our friend. I suggest we ask him for his help. Raise your hand if you agree with me.' The sea of raised hands answered his question.

'Motion passed. I will compose a note for Samuel this very evening. Then we must decide who can present it to him.' All eyes turned to Peter.

'Yes, I will do this. I will be happy to.' And with that the villagers left and the hall emptied in a fraction of the time it had taken to fill it.

****

The screech of the chalk on the blackboard woke Samuel from his daydream. He much preferred being in a dream, where he could follow whichever way the story took him, than in a classroom. The words from parents' evening still echoed in his ears though and helped serve to force his concentration back to the lesson. That and the screeching chalk.

Never had there been such a substance so guaranteed to set a person's teeth on edge than chalk. Strange that your teeth should feel the effects of the grating sound of chalk being dragged across a board, thought Samuel. He often questioned everyday things that others took for granted and chose not to ever question. This special trait and others of empathy, curiosity, compassion, were the reasons why the mayor had chosen Samuel to help the villagers of Safe Haven Village. News that he was needed in the book had not yet reached his ears.

So far, no method had been established whereby Samuel could make contact with the book when he was not in it, or that they, in turn, could make contact with him. Peter now found himself in a similar situation. He was desperate to pass the note from the mayor to Samuel and had no wish to wait until bedtime when Samuel would creep, exhausted and ready for sleep, inside the book between pages one and two.

This also meant that Peter would have the long trek through so many pages from Safe Haven Village all the way to the front of the book. The chances were that he would not reach Samuel before he fell asleep. He thought about the story Samuel had told him about little Hannah tripping and falling off the bottom of page 12. How she had appeared in a castle and how Samuel had returned her to page 12 and to her story. He had enjoyed the tale very much, partly because it was true and also because it had a happy ending.

What if? Ideas spun round Peter's head. *What if he could find a carrier pigeon, or a similar bird, within the book? A bird that would be willing to help the villagers of Safe Haven with no thought of reward for itself?*

No sooner had he put the thought out onto the universe, and it had become airborne, than a small bird appeared at Peter's right hand.

'I know I am small but not too small to carry a note. I heard the mayor speak. If I can somehow get out of the book – and back again – I will be able to give the note to Samuel and return safely.' Peter was quite used to talking birds because nothing was impossible in the make believe book.

'Let's try it! I will fasten the note to one of your legs and open the page of the book. If we can somehow muster up a strong wind, it could blow you out of the book.' The bird seemed satisfied with this. Before it had chance to grow nervous about the possibility of not returning, Peter quickly added 'Samuel can bring you back to the book with him. Just like he did with Hannah from page 12. It will all work very well.'

****

Samuel had lapsed into yet another daydream during a lesson intended to teach them French. The teacher was about to descend on him with pointed comments about 'daydreaming away his life' and 'school days are the best days of your life, you must spend them wisely'. Before she had chance to utter the first words, as predictable as they were wasted, a loud tapping sound was heard on the window pane. Everyone turned to look. A small bird seemed intent on breaking into the classroom, so fierce was its pecking, so intense its movements. Without logical thought, or indeed any idea what he planned to do, Samuel was on his feet racing towards the window. He opened it and in flew the bird to the excitement of the class and the utter dismay of the teacher.

'Samuel! Whatever possessed you to open the window?! Now we'll never be able to get rid of it.'

'Perhaps it's hungry Miss?' Jocelyn suggested. 'Hungry and thirsty?'

An assortment of food quickly surrounded the small bird that sat still, and apparently unafraid, on Samuel's desk. Someone had found an empty ink well and had filled it with water. This was perfect. The bird now had more than it could eat in one sitting and water to satisfy its thirst whenever it felt like it. Eventually, the chaos subsided and the little bird seemed to be nodding off on Samuel's desk. The lesson began where it left off with Samuel's classmates casting furtive glances at the bird. Samuel felt a sense of pride that the bird had chosen him to settle with.

He was half way through writing a list of French verbs when he noticed the note tied to one of the bird's legs. He managed to remove it without waking the bird who by now was in a deep slumber, having travelled further than any of them might have guessed.

Unfolding the note carefully, out of sight, Samuel learned the real reason for the arrival of the bird in his classroom. He was needed in the book. The villagers of Safe Haven needed his help. Now. There was no time to lose. He thought quickly; then it came to him in a flash. Feign illness.

'Miss. I don't feel very well,' he murmured, slumping forward as he spoke.

'What! Again? You've only just recovered from a fever. Your mother was telling me. Do you need to go home or can you hold on until the end of school?'

'I'd rather prefer to go home now,' Samuel persisted, trying not to appear too desperate by putting just the right amount of urgency in his voice.

'Alright,' Mrs Walters knew when she'd lost. 'I'll see if I can run you home in my car at lunch time. Is one of your parents able to look after you once you get there?'

'My father is working at home today.'

'Good. We'll have you there in no time.' Samuel gathered up his school books and packed them, or rather threw them, into his rucksack. The little bird he treated with rather more care. Offering his arm as a perch he strode purposefully to the waiting car with the bird held aloft like a mascot representing the winning team. His journey to the car was watched by dozens of classmates who bore witness to the strange sight of boy plus bird making their way to the car. It was a memory that would stay with them long into adulthood and indeed would resurface as a story to be told to their grandchildren in future times.

Once Samuel and his delicate travelling companion were safely installed in the back seat, the car sped off in the direction of Samuel's home. Mrs Walters, the teacher responsible for pastoral care, did not hang around. She focussed on getting the job done and got it done in a fraction of the time it would have taken anyone else. Efficiency could have been her middle name, so able was she to concentrate on what needed to be done, so unprepared to be distracted by unexpected happenings. Yet, despite an air of nonchalance and apparent indifference afforded to those around her, Mrs Walters was the most compassionate caring person you could ever hope to meet. As such, she was perfect in a crisis and the person everyone turned to whenever a crisis or emergency presented itself.

Mrs Walters waited in the car until she saw the front door open and a concerned face look down at Samuel, followed by a thankful wave of the hand in gratitude and to signify that there was no need for her to wait. All was in hand.

Having convinced his father that all he needed was a warm drink and a sleep in his bedroom, Samuel retreated upstairs. He felt almost tempted to make a sign saying 'Do not disturb' and hang it on his door. He resisted the urge though when he imagined his father's face. A mixture of concern and sadness. His father did not deserve such a dismissive statement and Samuel decided to take a chance. He would slip into the book, with the bird, in the middle of the day and hope that he would not be discovered, that his absence would go unnoticed.

Movement into the book was almost seamless. He and the bird found themselves on page one, Samuel's usual entry point, without so much as the wafting of a page. The bird was greatly relieved.

'Thank you Samuel but you must go now. I can find my own way back but you need to go to Safe Haven Village as fast as your legs can carry you.' As if he had wings attached to his heels, Samuel turned and flew off through the book.

He arrived in the village just as dusk was casting shadows on the hillside. He looked quickly towards the clock on the church tower. Already half past six and at this time of year darkness came quickly. Like a rip tide that crept up soundlessly and could isolate you in a rock cove on the beach so nightfall could do the same. It robbed you of your visual senses, cloaked familiar surroundings with the hand of night, hushed the animals in the wood and, worst of all for Samuel, made it almost impossible for him to track his way back to page one in the book.

He must act quickly if he was to be out of the book and appearing for his supper at half past seven. A hot drink and buttered toast that, should he not appear for it, would ring alarm bells and propel his parents into a flurry of anxious activity. They only had his well-being at heart, he knew that, but nevertheless Samuel rather wearied of the constant need for them to know where he was at any given time. He entered the village via the scenic route, a pathway lined with trees. Knocking on the first door drew out the occupants who, after initially expressing alarm, were overjoyed to see that they had Samuel in their midst.

'Any news Samuel? Any more ideas about how we can make rain and save our crops?' A weather-beaten woman looked up at him, desperation in her eyes. Samuel did not wish to admit that no ground-breaking plan had yet raised itself in his consciousness. He smiled a smile of hope and camaraderie as if to hint that very shortly a great idea would overwhelm him and save the crops of Safe Haven Village. Then, just as suddenly as he had accepted that no idea had surfaced in his mind, it came to him. An idea to triumph all others. He would ask birds to fly into the clouds. He had heard of cloud-seeding at school and, from the little he had understood, sending something into the midst of a cloud could trigger rain.

'We must talk to the birds. Please send a message out to all the birds in the book and ask them to come here as soon as they can.' The message was sent, the words spoken, the dye cast. So many birds took to the skies that they blocked out what little light was still filtering through from the sun.

As one they flew up into the middle of the biggest cloud that lay over the village. The eagle, being the biggest and the strongest, led the way. From the ground it appeared as if a large dark arrow was about to pierce the cloud. For a brief moment the birds vanished within the cloud, only to appear above it.

'They've flown right through the cloud,' cried Letitia. The birds returned to the surrounding trees and, with the villagers, watched the sky with baited breath. Samuel was counting silently, mouthing the words.

'One, two, three, four.....' He reached seventeen and then there was an almighty crash as thunder roared and lightning spiked the ground causing some villagers to jump into the air, startled and fearful. The light and sound display was followed immediately by a torrential downpour as the massive cloud emptied its entire contents over the village, the surrounding fields and the desperately dry, water-craving crops.

The bursting of this cloud seemed to trigger a neighbouring cloud to do the same and very soon rain was falling across the whole valley, from the top of the hills to the lower fields. Samuel had done it. The drought had ended. He had brought rain to Safe Haven Village.

There was now the small matter of finding his way home with night almost upon him. He was not left to dwell upon this as an eagle stepped into his path and offered his back. In no time at all Samuel was back on page one and slipping out of the book into his bedroom just in time for supper.

Chapter 13

The thief

There was a thief in the book. Someone had caught a brief glimpse of a dark shadow that leapt between pages clutching at words as he went and wreaking havoc amongst the stories. His nimble fingers grabbed at any vowels and consonants that he could lay his hands on, as well as entire words. In one story it was claimed that he had removed two complete sentences.

This was a sad state of affairs. No-one dared take their eyes off a word for a second. It seemed that the minute their back was turned yet another word had vanished from the page in an instant. The thief was indeed adept at his trade. The storybook characters referred to the thief as him but indeed no-one had any idea whether the perpetrator was male or female. All that had ever been seen was the fleeting glimpse of a pair of heels that flashed as the owner leapt to yet another page to escape the scene of a recent crime.

The entire book was awash with theories. Could it possibly be one of them? Surely not? If it was, how could the thief have got into the book? No-one suspected Samuel. He was their friend. The thought was there though that if Samuel had managed to get into the book then it was not impossible that other, less friendly, souls might have found their way there.

The chaos created was unfathomable and unheard of. Never, in the life of the book, had any part of a story gone missing. Now there appeared to be parts of every story that were noticeable by their absence, highlighted by intermittent, pristine, white sections that shone out from the page, like shafts of sunlight through trees that lined a road. And with the missing sections came a more sinister outcome.

Where a section of story had vanished, so too had some of the storybook characters. Others appeared to be stranded, stopped in the middle of doing something, frozen to the spot, unable to move on to their next task or adventure as the words were not there to spell out their next movements. This was the worst disaster to befall the book since the great storm of the last century. But that was another story. The question that was on everyone's lips was

'What was the thief planning to do with all the stolen words and sentences; in some cases entire paragraphs? What had he in store for them? And where was he keeping them all?'

'Give them back!' the words echoed down the wind that poured through the alleyways throughout the book. The united outpourings of the beleaguered villagers bereft at the loss of characters from their book. Not merely characters in terms of letters, but characters that made up the stories themselves, who were part of the story – who were the story.

Samuel was familiar with the phrase 'lost for words' taking it to mean that however hard a person might be searching for a particular word or phrase, it constantly eluded them, dodging this way and that as they desperately sought to lay their hands on it and claim it for their own. In the case of the stolen words, missing from the book, the opposite had happened. A thief had run away with the words, rather than the other way round.

Samuel was honoured to be asked to help in the search but mystified as to who might have taken the words or indeed why? He had climbed the never-ending stairs to the top of the spire that crowned the church in Safe Haven Village, thinking that the bracing air might instil some ideas into him.

The wind tugged insistently at his collar, pulling it this way and that, as if urging him to make a decision. His hair, that was never tidy, now appeared more unruly than ever and blew across his face triumphantly, impairing his already challenged vision. Samuel gazed into the distance and could vaguely make out the hillside on page 12 where currently only Hannah rested half way down.

Dick was missing from her side. With the removal of the letters, D and I, had come the removal of Dick, her brother, and companion in all things.

Samuel turned to the East and saw only rolling hills kissed by clouds that bumbled across the sky in an unhurried fashion. Where, in all this land, could the thief have taken the stolen words? Maybe he had not chosen only one site to hide them. Maybe he had left them at many different places along the way. They could be hidden under logs, scurried away in a squirrel nut hole, buried inside a badger sett. The list of places was endless and Samuel had no idea where to start. As luck would have it time was on his side. It was half-term holiday with no school for one week.

He thought long and hard, then, with the sun sinking in the sky, began the long descent down the steps of the spire. 'All things come to those who wait.' A well-used proverb. If there was any truth in it, an idea would come to Samuel and all could be put right. The mayor had explained to him that 'time is of the essence'. And so it was that Samuel, back in his bedroom, began to put pen to paper and write idly, in the vain hope that inspiration would come to him either in his waking hours or during sleep. An idea would present itself that would identify in an instant how the lost words could be retrieved and the book made whole again.

****

Someone was sweeping with a stiff broom. The long handle waved to and fro. It was being held at the bottom by a small person barely able to wield such a large object. He was sweeping away leaves that had strayed too far from the tree. Carefully, and with the utmost concentration, the leaves were being methodically swept into a bucket laid on its side.

Peter happened to be passing and leant on a nearby gate, watching the activity with idle curiosity. As a raven watches for a glint amongst gathered leaves, or a magpie detects treasure in a pile of rubbish, Peter spotted something unusual in the leaves. He blinked to clear his vision, in case he had been deceived and all that lay before him was worthless and of no real interest once fully recovered.

No, there it was again, a flash of black amongst the dried red-brown leaves. A little squiggle that suggested nothing concrete or recognisable to Peter's discerning eyes but raised his curiosity nonetheless. He leaned away from the gate and lightly trawled his boot through the leaves.

'Hey! Watch it!' came the angry retort. 'It's taken me ages to gather up these leaves and now you're messing it all up. Destroying my work. Wasting my efforts.' Peter drew back, murmuring words of apology.

'Didn't mean to. Just helping Samuel to look for the lost letters.' At this the elf that was pushing the broom dropped it and stood to attention with a rapt expression on his face.

'The missing words?! You think the missing words might be here amongst the leaves?' The voice was slight but hurried.

'I'm not sure. Do you mind if I have a closer look?' asked Peter.

Together they searched the leaf pile. Carefully turning it over revealed something that, on closer inspection, proved to be a single letter, the capital 'E'. Further investigation turned up more letters and even a couple of words. They laid them out on the ground, trying to make sense of the seemingly unrelated characters but, however they placed them, no sense could be made of it, no meaning revealed.

'They could have come from very different parts of the book,' suggested the elf and Peter agreed. 'How might we get them back into the book when we don't know where they came from?' the elf continued.

'Let's think about how they arrived here in the first place, shall we?' said Peter, answering the elf's question with a question of his own. 'They were here in the leaves. Laid on the ground. Apparently unheeded and ignored. But what if they had been stored here on purpose and you had just happened upon them by accident? What then?'

The elf's brow furrowed in a deep concentrated frown.

'I think squirrels sometimes hide their nuts here amongst the leaves. Maybe the thief used the squirrel's hiding place and took it for his own.' It seemed like a reasonable possibility and they both sat, face in hands, trying to decide on the next move.

'How to return the characters back to the book,' the elf repeated. Then he jumped up. 'I have it. We wait for a flurry of wind, a kaleidoscope of rustling air that sweeps through the trees and lifts light things into the air.'

'You mean we should throw the letters and words into the wind?' asked Peter, confused.

'Not the wind. Not any wind,' corrected the elf. 'The four winds,' he said, with emphasis on the 'four'. 'We throw the characters to the four winds and let them take them home to their rightful place in the book.'

They sat silently and waited, having shared the characters between them, and clutched them tightly in their hands. A noise from the upper reaches of the trees brought their attention to the gathering force of a breeze as it swirled round them, tossing leaves hither and thither.

'We must catch exactly the right moment,' cautioned the elf. 'I know these winds of old. We must catch them unawares. Before the four winds will come the one we call 'the force of reason'. This is the wind we want.'

'How will we know?' asked Peter.

'I will know and I will tell you when it comes.' The swirling leaves continued and suddenly the elf shouted 'Now!' and simultaneously he and Peter flung the characters into the centre of the blustery air and to the four winds. They watched with bated breath as the centre of the wind storm flung the letters and words about in all directions, North, South, East and West in turn, then, without an ounce of deliberation, the four winds drew them away.

The two let their breath out and looked at each other. They would have to hope that all was well and that the characters found their rightful places and inserted themselves back in the book. Time would tell. It was a great leveller and all would be revealed – in time....

That evening, in the square at Safe Haven Village, the mayor once again gathered the villagers together. A town crier was not necessary. Word spread quickly by word of mouth. It was not necessary to ring a bell.

'A wondrous thing has happened,' he began. 'Some characters have returned to the book. Odd letters to make sense of broken words. Odd words to complete sentences and restore their meaning.' The crowd murmured their relief and jubilation.

'I have it on good authority that Peter and elf Douglas acted out of wisdom and cunning. They found some hidden characters and tricked the four winds into returning them to the book. Now we have to find the others. This is just the beginning. It will not be an easy thing to do but we are on the way. The journey to making our book whole again has begun.'

The search for the missing words seemed endless. No stone was left unturned, no passing remark ignored, no path left untrodden. Every effort was made. The whole village was striving to achieve the seemingly impossible. Since the chance find of a few letters, and a couple of words amongst a heap of leaves, no further discoveries had been made. Spirits were low, hopes fading, lives disrupted. Many families had lost one member to the thief who had dared to trawl the book for any letter or word that took his fancy. Words that held the name or spirit of a character in a story, held their very essence too, and with their vanishing came the disappearance of the person.

Twin boys were being cared for by their grandmother after their mother went missing at the very moment that the word that formed her name was stolen from her story. It was a wholly unacceptable state of affairs. Samuel had lain awake at night, in the book, trying to pull ideas out of thin air, but so far – nothing. He ventured to ask his closest school friend, Jocelyn.

'If you wanted to hide letters or words from stories in a book, where would you hide them?' he asked.

'You mean where would I hide them within the book? If I was able to actually get inside it?'

'Yes. Where do you think you might hide them so that no-one could see them on first looking? They would not be obviously there on the page.'

'Well.....' Jocelyn pondered. 'I would either hide them in a very secret place where I thought no-one would look, ever, or I would hide them in plain sight. I would put them somewhere where they were in full view and people passed them daily, but no-one realised they were stolen words.' Samuel looked at Jocelyn with admiration.

'That's amazing. I never thought of that.'

'But..' Jocelyn continued, 'it all depends on why the thief took the words or letters in the first place and what they plan to use them for. Did they want to upset people in the book, out of a sense of spite or revenge, or did they have a personal reason for wanting to own some extra words – words of their own that they could do as they wished with.' Without knowing it Jocelyn had hit on the truth. The thief did indeed have his own personal reason for wanting to take words and letters for his own use. He had great expectations. He was planning his own book.

Chapter 14

Disruption

For some time now the thief had been deliberating on how best to hit on a good story line, something that would prove irresistible, that would draw people to read it and be unable to put it down. But, however hard he thought, the ideas were not forthcoming, inspiration eluded him, the words would just not come. And without the words the thief had no story. He must have words. It was then that the seed of an idea began to germinate in his mind. If the words would not come to him, to allow him to write a story of great merit and fascination, then he must look elsewhere for them. Places other than within his own mind, which appeared to be barren of ideas and interesting concepts and, indeed, words.

The thief was a Will o' the Wisp sort of figure who lived between books and the world of humans and faeries. It was no problem for him to be able to enter and leave a book at will and it was only a matter of time before he found himself drawing his fingers lightly over the leather-bound volume that graced Samuel's bedside table.

This was a book of some standing. A book above all others where the storyline drew the reader in from the very first sentence, captivating them and leading them deeper into the book and making it virtually impossible to put down. What the thief did not know, however, was that the book was a living thing. Not merely an inanimate object containing words starkly printed on a page.

The words in this book, as in all books, formed the characters in the stories. Characters who lived out their own lives when the book was closed and not being read. He could not have known that each letter and word that he lifted from a page, without thought or consideration, would alter, in a profound way, the lives of the story book people.

He had not thought it through and after he had prised the first few words from their sentence, and individual letters from the words, he stood gazing down at what he held in his hands. He could not have realised that here, held within these words, was the life blood of the book and that through his acts of wanton vandalism he was destroying the very soul of the book.

The thief had not even given any thought to where he was going to store the words and letters, until he could begin to fit them all together to make his own book, his own story. Some he hid in rabbit burrows, others in badger setts or amongst leaves.

Others, still, he took to placing in plain sight where they could be seen by anyone passing by, if only they had been aware of them. It is a fact that people tend not to see the obvious and the thief used this to his advantage. So many places were perfect hiding places for the stolen letters. A little poster advertising a village dance suddenly suffered from a surfeit of letters. Anyone who might have noticed would probably have put this down to poor spelling on the part of the poster writer.

Milestones, at cross roads within the book, suddenly gained a few more letters. These adorned the inscribed destination in a way that served to both puzzle and mystify the traveller who began to question whether they were travelling in the right direction after all. Yes, hiding letters in plain sight appeared to be working well for the thief; that is until Jocelyn had her bright idea. Samuel would go into the book that night with a plan that would illuminate all their efforts to find the missing pieces of text and restore them to where they belonged – in the book.

****

Evening could not come fast enough for Samuel. His mother noticed his agitated movements and inability to sit still.

'What's the matter Samuel? Can't you settle?' she asked.

'No, I'm fine,' he replied. 'I'm just a bit tired.' To his mother he looked the opposite of tired but she decided not to say anything. Whatever was worrying her son was best left for him to sort out. If he needed her help he would ask for it, she told herself. Still, she couldn't help but feel a twinge of concern as she watched Samuel's retreating figure as he trod the stairs to his bedroom.

'Sleep tight,' she shouted after him. But the words failed to reach Samuel before the bedroom door closed behind him, shutting them out in a defining action that was both unintentional and final.

In less than a minute Samuel had changed into his 'book clothes'. These consisted of pyjamas hidden underneath jeans and a jumper with a waterproof coat on top of them. This combination worked well, Samuel had found, as he could travel through the book in reasonably normal attire without raising the suspicions of other book dwellers. He was also prepared for the eventuality of rain and, when the time came to sleep, he only had to remove the top layers to be instantly ready for bed. It was a carefully thought-out plan that he had tried and tested and it worked a treat.

Samuel flew through the book to Safe Haven Village as fast as his legs would carry him, sending the Humming bird ahead with a message for Peter and Letitia to alert them to his imminent arrival.

As he rounded the corner he saw ahead the village square. It was largely empty. There was no gathered throng hanging on the words of the mayor today.

Samuel, Peter and Letitia sat at the little round oak table in Peter's small house and Jocelyn's idea was discussed.

'So we need to look for letters and words hidden in plain sight?' Letitia concluded.

'Yes. Shall we start right now?' The three moved out into the lane by the house and looked around, not having an inkling which direction to take.

'Let us check anything at all we come across that has writing on it,' suggested Samuel. 'Look at that poster over there by the village shop, for instance. At first glance it looks fine but now I look at it more closely I can see that all is not quite right. All is not as it should be. It doesn't scan properly.' They walked across and Samuel touched the words with his fingertips, which gave him a better idea of what was happening.

'My sight seems to be better when I am in the book, for some reason, but I can still discover a great deal more from touching things,' he explained. 'Here, this is a letter that has been stuck on the poster and has not been merely printed on the sheet of paper.' Every time Samuel's fingers came upon a raised object he peeled it away and laid it on the ground.

Shortly he seemed satisfied that all added letters or words had been removed and he stood back from the poster. They gazed in amazement. There, arranged higgledy-piggledy on the ground were eleven separate letters and four complete words. They gathered them up and put them carefully in the bread container in Peter's house.

'We must tell the mayor,' said Letitia.

'Or would it not be better to return them to the book as I did with the first set of found letters and words?' asked Peter.

'Yes, I think that would be a good idea,' Letitia smiled and Samuel nodded. 'But let us make a note of what we have here before we release them to the four winds.' They set to, busily searching for a piece of paper on which to inscribe the characters. Then they went in search of the four winds.

Today the four winds were nowhere to be found. Like a butterfly flitting from plant to plant they constantly eluded the three who sought them. They looked under bushes, in tunnels, round the corners of buildings. Anywhere where wind would normally catch you unawares, blowing your hat off, scattering your belongings, searing your face with its fresh coldness and blustery ways. Today the winds were lying low.

With no wind in sight the three had no option but to seek out a hiding place, a stronghold for the found characters, until they could be returned to the book. Where though? Hiding them in plain sight was not a good idea as they, themselves, had already discovered some hidden in this way. If they had foiled the thief, so might others. They would have to think very carefully indeed before placing them in safe keeping.

'Why not take them back to your world?' suggested Peter. 'There is less chance of them being discovered by the wrong people.'

'Good idea,' agreed Letitia. 'Let me look for something to hold them in and keep them safe for the time being.' Her eyes rested on a small leather satchel, not unlike the one that Samuel used to carry his books to school.

'This looks ideal don't you think?' Letitia sought approval in the faces of her companions.

'Absolutely,' Samuel said. The words and stray letters were duly wrapped and the satchel fastened and placed in Samuel's hand as, with the other hand, he fastened his coat buttons.

Chapter 15

The fireflies

Samuel awoke to a misty morning, with leaves laced with spiders' webs and dew drops. He had managed to take the satchel back to his bedroom the night before and store it safely in his wardrobe, before climbing back into the book once more to sleep.

Now back in his room ready to take on the day, and anything it had to offer, Samuel was thinking hard about where he could store the precious parcel of letters and words. It was only for the daylight hours until he could search again for the four winds once evening fell and shadows graced the pages of the book. He decided that they were best left in the wardrobe and headed off to school.

A nature trail was planned for the morning. They had all been shown photographs and plaster casts of footprints made by native British mammals and Samuel was fairly confident that he could identify a badger and a fox with ease. The badger because it had such an unusually large footprint, though this could easily be confused with that of a big dog. The fox as its footprints appeared as a single track, almost as if a creature with only one leg had made the prints. Squirrel prints were quite easy to learn as the two larger hind prints lay behind and to the side of the front paw prints. They had also been taught the habitat where each species could be found.

Wherever he was, and whatever he was doing, Samuel always had half a mind on the book. He found himself wondering what everyone was getting up to in his absence. As such his mind wandered easily, searching out the leafy lanes that drew the traveller towards Safe Haven Village.

'Samuel, are you with us?' his teacher gently asked. 'Do you know what we have been talking about?' Samuel had to admit that he had actually no idea what was being discussed in the classroom.

'Jocelyn, would you like to explain to Samuel the plan for today's trip out?' Jocelyn, Samuel's close friend at school, felt like a traitor but had been backed into a corner and had no choice but to repeat the words of Mrs Walters. When she'd finished she looked apologetically at Samuel and mouthed 'sorry'. She need not have worried. Samuel did not blame her in the slightest. He really must learn to concentrate more in lessons. If only he could develop two-way concentration so that he could think about the book and be part of the lesson at the same time. If only.....

The nature trip was good fun. They had spotted some badger footprints in the ground leading to a slow-running stream alongside a footpath that bordered a field. Even with their impaired eyesight it was easy to spot the break in the foliage where badgers had broken cover and come into the open to drink from the stream.

In some cases the prints made overnight had held fast and become sealed into the clay soil so that the children had been able to make a plaster cast of some of them. Samuel had been able to bring his home. His fingers stroked the cast of the footprints and felt the indentation where the badger had pressed its weight into the clay. The cast was the reverse of the paw print but to Samuel they were one and the same. The badger had made the print that had resulted in the plaster cast he held in his hands and that was good enough for him.

He thought about taking it into the book with him this evening, but decided against it. He had enough to carry and besides he might lose the plaster cast. No, better to add it to his little box of treasures and keep it out of harm's way. Samuel stopped breathing for a moment when he realised what had just passed through his mind. 'Out of harm's way.' He had never thought of the book as being a dangerous place to visit, but it was not totally without risk. Hannah had once fallen out of the book, and now a thief was running amok through the pages, hither and thither, lifting letters and words as he felt like it.

No regard for the lives of those left behind, lives that his very actions were disrupting. No thought at all. It just would not do and Samuel vowed to stop it.

Just before he had entered the book that evening he had looked out of the window and seen dotted lights on the hillside. They reminded him of something he had once seen in a book, one of those books that you could interact with by virtue of raised, three-dimensional structures that open up when the page is opened. One of these showed fireflies and glow worms. There was an explanation in large print describing what they were and pictures that lit up when you pressed a button on the page. What if he could call on the fireflies in the book to help in the search for the missing characters?

As Samuel moved through the book this evening, on his way to Safe Haven Village, he took his time. He sought out the stolen words and letters on each page as he went and leisurely took in his surroundings. He would like to get to know more of the people in the book but his task made this impossible at the moment. 'Time is of the essence,' the mayor had said. After Samuel had solved the desperate problem of drought in the village his esteem had risen to great heights and there was nothing that the others thought that he couldn't do. It was going to be hard to live up to their expectations.

'Fireflies!' Samuel's first words on arriving at Safe Haven Village took Peter and Letitia by surprise. 'We can ask the fireflies to help us in our search. They could fly low over hollows and other dark spots in the countryside or towns and throw some light on them. They could illuminate places where the missing words and letters might be found.'

'Brilliant. Just brilliant,' said Peter and Samuel beamed with pride.

'We can send out a message now,' said Letitia. 'I will do it by tapping on a branch, like Morse code, only using vibrations to carry the message rather than sound.'

'Perfect,' said Samuel. Within half an hour the light from thousands of fireflies could be seen twinkling in the valley below, and throughout every dark nook and cranny that existed in the village. Extra help was quickly gathered and little figures flitted about following the light provided by the fireflies.

The mission was remarkably successful. They stood around in the village square gazing down at the multitude of letters and words that had been collected.

'I will make a note of them all like before,' said Samuel. 'We need to know how many have been collected and how many are still missing. Then we need to find the four winds.'

'There is just one problem.' Everyone turned to stare at Peter. 'We are returning these characters to their rightful place in the book but what is to stop the thief from stealing them again? How do we know that he has stopped his stealing spree?'

'We don't,' Samuel said slowly. 'To put an end to all this, for all time, we need to catch the thief.'

'Shouldn't we keep these found letters and words safely with the others then, for now – and only return them back to the book when we have caught him?' Samuel counted his blessings, not for the first time, for having such loyal and inspiring friends.

'Yes, we must do exactly that. We must find the thief first.'

****

'Tread softly. Stay in the shadows. Keep to myself. Avoid strangers.' The thief was muttering to himself as he crept along the side of a building, down a cobbled path. He was disgruntled and out of sorts. Some of the letters and words that he had gone to great lengths to remove from the page and store in hidden places, far from prying eyes, had gone missing. Stranger still, some had reappeared on the very page that he had prised them from in the first place.

He did not think that the people from Safe Haven Village, nor indeed the entire book, were clever enough to have achieved this on their own. But the thief was wrong. Never misjudge other people. If you should take gentleness for stupidity, or kindness for misplaced trust, you will live to see the error of your judgement. He was right, however, to think that the story book characters had had help in their endeavour to reclaim what had been taken from them and what was rightfully theirs.

When the thief first noticed the reappearance of some words, that he knew for sure he had stolen, he was flabbergasted. He even checked to see that they were indeed the same ones that he had taken. Strangely enough, when he tried to prise them from their position a second time, they refused to co-operate. He pushed with all his might, this way and that, and still they refused to budge.

The thief was more surprised than he was irritated by his failure. If Peter, Letitia and Samuel had known about the failure of the letters to be easily moved from the page, at this second attempt at stealing, that the letters were resisting the efforts of the thief, they would have breathed a sigh of relief. They would have gone, once more, in search of the four winds, to return the rest of their ever-growing hoard to the pages they were stolen from.

But they were not aware that the effort they had used when sticking letters back in the book had been successful to the point where they were now almost impossible to remove from the page. Though they did not yet know it, they were thwarting the thief in his endeavour to steal the same words twice.

The villagers, and indeed the occupants of the whole book, were on high alert. They knew to look out for, and to report, anyone who seemed to be acting suspiciously. This was not an easy task as all the characters looked on each other as family. What was simple to do, however, was to be able to spot a stranger. Anyone who was not 'one of them' could be detected at a distance even in dimming light. Even their silhouette would register instantly as unfamiliar. Despite this no suspects had so far raised their head and the thief remained as elusive as ever.

> 'Slowly does it,
> Watch your step,
> Keep to the shadows,
> Don't look back.'

Letitia had devised a sort of mantra that she muttered to herself when out searching for the thief. She found that Samuel had added to it:

> 'Two steps forward
> One step back
> Never falter
> Stay on track'

The three of them, Peter included, found that this helped them to focus on the job in hand and not to deviate from their chosen task, or lose their concentration.

'We have looked everywhere,' Letitia sighed in dismay. 'We must have covered every inch of the book.'

'Yes, perhaps,' replied Samuel. 'But not every single nook and cranny, even though the fireflies helped tremendously.' Peter nodded sagely and looked to the lit windows of a house nearby. The curtains were being drawn and at that moment a shadow crossed behind them. A silhouette that alerted Peter.

'Is it possible that the thief is not a real person like us, but a shadow – like Peter Pan's shadow?' Samuel gasped.

'You could be right. What an incredible idea. Maybe we should look for a shadow.' They set off again, with new purpose and intent, on the trail of the thief, watching for any shadow that lingered a little longer than it might, looked a little more different than might be expected. The hunt was renewed.

****

The thief had not always been so. He had been known as Matthias before mischief and disaster befell him. Now he was a thief. He took good care of his shadow. In fact that was all that was left of him. There was once a time when he had been a whole person and could be seen by all he passed. But the thief had been careless. One day he had tripped when edging his way across a wooden fence over a brook. His shadow had torn away from his foot and, like a ball of wool that unravels the further away you move from it, so did his shadow separate from his body. It peeled away much like a snake sheds its skin.

By the time he had reached the far side of the brook, and run nimbly up the hill, it was too late. Only when he looked round and noticed that all the trees and flowers were casting shadows, and he was not, did he realise that something was seriously amiss. To be without your shadow in the land of make believe was nothing short of a disaster. True, it meant that he could creep up on unsuspecting beings and surprise them but it was not in his nature to do this.

Matthias was a peaceful, quiet little chap who went about his life untroubled, and generally minded his own business. If anyone was in need he was eager to do what he could to help. Above all, it was not in his nature to steal. Indeed nothing could be further from his mind. His parents had taught him to 'do unto others as you would like others to do unto you'. It was a bit of a mouthful to remember and indeed it had been some time before he had fully understood the message that the little saying was intended to convey.

How could he retrieve his shadow? It was of the utmost importance to him. Where was it anyway? He had retraced his steps but seen no sign of it.

Nothing that resembled the tail-end of a shirt hanging over the fence that crossed the brook. Nothing. Surely it could not have gone off on its own? But the instant this thought crossed his mind he knew it to be true. His shadow had indeed gone off on its own.

Having been attached to Matthias for its entire life, it was now experiencing freedom for the first time. Matthias was finding it difficult to understand what had happened. He had thought that the shadow could not possibly exist without him. They were one and the same. If anything the shadow needed him more than he needed the shadow. Without Matthias there to stand at the correct angle to the sun or the moon there could be no shadow. But again, this logical conclusion did not calm the ever-growing anxious and agitated thoughts that were jumbling around and vying for position in his mind. And what could the shadow get up to without his calming influence? He was soon to find out.

Almost with his tail between his legs, had he had a tail, he retreated to a deep, hidden part of the forest to feel sorry for himself and to work out a plan to retrieve his shadow. The shadow, in the meantime, also lay low for a while, working out its next move. It was enjoying its freedom and had no wish to be captured and sealed back in position, trailing round after the little figure that was Matthias, its every movement dictated.

The shadow decided to go on a spree. Venturing inside an unattended book, lying on a small boy's bedside table, it discovered a world of words and, in a momentous decision borne of ambition, aspiration, greed and devilment, it decided to gather words to form its own book. The shadow that had no body to belong to was now forging a new career as a story writer and a thief. This book would hold no original thoughts and ideas, but contain only stolen words, for this would be the work of a thief.

Chapter 16

Day of reckoning

The thief had been having a field day stealing letters, words, and even entire sentences, whenever the mood took him. At no time did he ever think that he might be creating a bad reputation for the shadow-less figure that was Matthias, now dwelling deep in the forest. Anyone who recognised the shadow's silhouette as belonging to Matthias, would jump to the conclusion that the shadow and Matthias were one and the same; that Matthias had become a thief. Much muttering and gasps of disbelief had been heard in the book when someone had first recognised the shadow of Matthias.

'Isn't that Matthias's shadow?' someone asked. 'It couldn't be him that is stealing from our book could it?'

'Not possible,' said another.

'He is normally such an inoffensive little chap. Keeps himself to himself,' said another. But in time they had all come to face the harsh truth of the matter. The shadow did indeed belong to Matthias. What they did not know, however, was that Matthias no longer belonged to the shadow. It was unattached

111

and acting of its own volition.

The thief, alias the shadow of Matthias, had made a decision to be bad. It was not something that had befallen him by chance. He had made a conscious decision to go about his own selfish way, with total disregard for anyone but himself. When the shadowless figure, that was Matthias, discovered this, his task would be to try to reverse the decision made by his shadow. Until he could secure the shadow and reattach it to himself, he must somehow try to change the attitude of the shadow. To do this he must enlist the help of the other characters in the book.

Poor Matthias, hidden away in the forest, planning his next move, was yet to learn about the thefts from the book and the efforts being made to retrieve the stolen words. Only when the fireflies descended on the dark hollow where he was hiding did he get a glimmer of what was happening. In an act of bravery he decided he must come out of the forest and clear his name – at all costs.

****

Matthias had seen this tree before. He spun round and examined the forest closely. Yes, he had been walking in a circle. His first venture so deep into the forest had led him into unchartered territory. He had lost his bearings and needed help. But who could he trust? What about Letitia? She had always been a true friend to him. He would call upon a bird to send a message to Letitia. The bird of wisdom and swiftness, a Kestrel, could take a note attached to its leg, much like the bird who had carried a note to Samuel in his classroom when they were troubled by the drought.

Matthias kept the words simple. 'I have lost my shadow and I am lost in the deep forest. Please help me. The bird knows where I am.'

The Kestrel flew fast and true towards its goal. As she read the note Letitia's hand flew to her mouth.

'Matthias is lost in the deep forest,' she gasped. 'We must let the bird take us to him.' Without an ounce of hesitation she and Peter drew their cloaks round them and ran as fast as they could, trying to keep the Kestrel in their sights as they did so. It was not an easy task. The ground was stony and once or twice they tripped and had to be helped to their feet by the other.

'I wish we could run faster,' Letitia fretted. 'We are losing the light. Soon it will be dark and we will never find Matthias without light to show us the way.

'We could call on the fireflies,' suggested Peter and, as before, the fiery insects came to their rescue, aided by a full moon that brightened the sky and flooded each dark crevice with a shining brightness where nothing could remain hidden for long.

****

113

'Skip one, jump one,
Leap to the side
There is nowhere in this book
Where letters they can hide
On the page they lie so flat
Hidden in full view
For me to steal and carry off
To pastures far and new.'

The shadow chanted his little rhyme, pleased with how it sounded and thrilled with how easy his task was turning out to be. Gather as many letters and words as he could to begin to build his new book. No matter that the book would have no note of originality about it, no ounce of newness delivered by itself, no streak or flash of inspiration that had arrived through him in the dead of night.

What the shadow did not realise was that satisfaction and a sense of achievement only come as a result of hard work and perseverance. Through a sense of knowing that you had kept on to the bitter end. Had struggled against adversity, had not let illness or tiredness get in the way or impede the journey to the final goal.

The shadow did not understand the fact that success could only really be experienced if you had expended some effort and worked to the best of your ability. It had to be earned.

The shadow was also lacking in empathy for his fellow beings and had felt no remorse when he had left Hannah alone on the hillside without Dick by her side, her companion in all things. Without an ounce of compassion he had callously removed the letters, D and I, from the word that formed his name and, in so doing, had removed Dick, Hannah's brother, from the page and hence the story.

The shadow was lacking in compassion as this side of his personality, when he was whole, lay with Matthias. It was now up to him to try to instil in his shadow the very senses that were currently lacking. Senses that also included awareness of your fellow beings, your companions on the journey through life.

****

It was going to be an uphill struggle but Letitia was prepared. No sooner had she untied the note from the leg of the Kestrel than a plan had begun to form. They reached the deep forest and hugged Matthias before bringing him back to Safe Haven Village for a warm drink. He told his story and they listened patiently until every last thread of the story had been untangled and laid bare.

'So,' began Letitia. 'There are three things we must do. Get the shadow to feel compassion and encourage it to return the lost letters and words of its own free will. Then we must unite you, Matthias, with your shadow.'

'That seems the best way forward,' said Peter. 'I'm sure Samuel would agree. It is not enough just to find stolen words and put them back in the book only for the shadow to steal them again. That will not do!'

'No, not at all,' agreed Matthias, beginning to revive in front of the roaring coal fire in Peter's little house. 'And I can clear my name. That is so important to me,' he said, his little face looking sad and downcast as he spoke.

'Absolutely,' Peter said. 'We will clear your name and restore the book. Now we must find Samuel.'

****

The day at school had not gone well. There was no smooth pathway from porridge at breakfast to the walk home along the path by the woods. Unforeseen events had marred the day, disturbing the natural order of things. A new person had arrived in Samuel's class. It was not that he felt animosity towards the new member of the school, more that he didn't trust him.

He could not quite put his finger on what bothered him about the new addition to his class. On the surface of things Alexander, for that was his name, appeared to be nothing out of the ordinary, but when Samuel was staring at the blackboard, trying his best to concentrate on the lesson, he knew that he was being watched.

He felt eyes burning into him, as if someone was trying to search his mind for anything of interest, a clue that it could use to its own advantage. But every time Samuel looked quickly to his left, where Alexander was seated, at a desk in line with his own, no face returned his stare. Alexander was looking intently at the board. Samuel was absolutely sure though that he was being watched or, if not watched, that something was out to do mischief and disturb his thoughts and general sense of well-being.

The school day ended and Samuel and Jocelyn, his close friend, made their way to the gates. As it was such a short journey home and darkness was not yet upon them, it was considered safe enough for the children to make their own way. Samuel turned out of the school gate and bid farewell to Jocelyn before setting off in the direction of home. In two minutes he had reached the edge of the dark wood and could see the familiar chimneys and bordering wall of his parents' house beckoning to him beyond the wood.

Like Safe Haven Village felt like to the villagers who lived there, inside the book, so this house served as a symbol of security and contentment, a welcoming beacon on the landscape, a place of sanctuary. He stood there for a few brief seconds gazing at the house and then went to move forwards but something stopped him.

Something resisted his efforts to walk on. Puzzled, he looked down at his boots, then at his coat sleeve. A hand rested on his arm and was tugging at him. Samuel tried to throw off the hand that held him, but it continued to hold him fast. With his other hand he fought to free himself from what seemed like an iron grip. Panic overwhelmed him. Like a cloud creeps over the top of a mountain and gradually envelops it, a feeling of fear, dismay and dread descended over him and he felt an icy clench round his heart. He fought with every inch of his being, as if his very life depended on it. Then he turned and shouted.

'What do you want with me? Who are you?' But no-one stood there beside him. His arm, inside his coat sleeve, was still held fast, as if by an invisible hand.

'Show yourself you coward!' cried Samuel, half out of annoyance, half out of desperation. Then, like a photograph magically appears when a film is being developed, first a hand, then an arm, then an entire body gradually materialised and Samuel recognised instantly the new arrival in his class at school, Alexander.

'How dare you grab me and stop me in my tracks!' Samuel was most indignant and also relieved to see that it was a human and not anything else that had waylaid him. Assuming, of course, that Alexander was human.....

'I'm very sorry to stop you like this. I could see no other way. Like you I am a book traveller and I wanted to speak to you urgently. I had to get you on your own to ask for your help.'

'How did you make yourself invisible?' asked Samuel intrigued.

'I didn't. Not really. You didn't see me partly because you were not expecting to. I have the ability to vanish in plain sight. It's quite easy when you know how. I kept a low profile, trod softly, stayed in the shadows. I knew that you, like me, cannot see well when the light is low. We have that in common. But let me tell you my story and why I need your help.'

Samuel listened as Alexander told him about letters, and even whole words, being taken randomly from books all over the city. The word-thief was not just causing havoc in his own bedside book. He was ruining stories all over the place and upsetting the bedtime reading of many children. Samuel explained what he knew and what steps were being taken to solve the problem in his own book. He referred to it as his book as that is how he thought of it, his very own book.

Alexander was greatly relieved to hear that a plan was already underway and Samuel promised to let him know what progress had been made, once he had spent the approaching night in the book. He would report back to Alexander the next morning and arrangements were made to meet at the same spot.

'But promise me that you will be waiting in full view, not invisible like today?' Samuel asked, and his new friend nodded.

Chapter 17

The words fight back

The thief was beginning to have a change of heart. The initial thrill gained from rustling words and letters from the pages of books, and hiding them away in secret places, was starting to fade. To add to this feeling that all was not as satisfying as it used to be was the fact that he had no-one to share his conquests with. No face full of anticipation longing to listen to details of his latest exploits. Being a thief on his own was not turning out to be a good experience.

He also had the growing sensation that something was missing from him. So far he had not been able to work out what this might be. At first he thought it might just be a growing disenchantment with life, brought on by the relentless repetition of the events of each day. Days which seemed to roll into one in a seamless, unending roll of boredom that was starting to annoy him to the point of desperation.

Then, one day, it gradually began to dawn on him. Could it be that part of him was missing? That he had lost it somewhere along the way? Been careless to the point of stupidity? And what might he have lost? He checked his fingers and toes. All there.

Everything intact. But one day the sun crept behind a cloud and the thief vanished, for there was no body there to produce a shadow. It was then that the thief knew. If he was only a shadow part of the time, he must have lost the part of him that produced the shadow – a body.

The words had decided to fight back. There had been a growing unrest across the book, moving from page to page. Slowly at first then gathering a pace as each page in turn took up the baton and ran with it. This was not wholly unexpected for these were magical letters and words that held within them the very spirit of the book and the essence of all of the characters. Each letter that was removed from a word, destroyed the ethos and meaning of the word and removed the item or person that the word represented.

'Stick ourselves down on the page,' murmured one word.

'Seal ourselves so that we cannot be removed,' said another.

'Resist being stolen,' yet another.

'We must present a united front, a show of strength,' offered one word; the word, 'Eloquence', astute as always and excellent at presenting a case in as clear and concise a manner as possible.

And so it was that the thief found himself on a page within the book one Sunday morning. Poised lightly, on the sheet of paper that he had sprung onto, he looked to the left and then the right deciding which letters to pounce upon first. Then he leapt into action. With deft fingers he tried to lift a letter from the page. No luck. Somewhat surprised he then tried to prise the letter away from its position exerting more pressure as he did so. Still no luck. Only after the thief had resorted to using a sharp piece of wood did the letter finally succumb to the efforts of the thief. It reluctantly gave itself up into the hands that were eager to take it and add it to the ever-growing hoard of stolen words.

The sudden resistance of letters and words, to being taken, took the thief by surprise. On one occasion he was left speechless, the irony of which did not escape him, considering that it was his actions that had left many stories within the book without meaning and rendered many of the characters lost in space. A space outside the book. In limbo. He was also starting to feel less confident and less sure that he was doing the right thing. It seemed such a great challenge, full of excitement, to begin with; to steal a few characters and to write his own book. But what had once been something to strive for now seemed like a millstone round his neck. An uphill struggle with undesirable undertones.

Night after night the thief sat and looked at the jumbled letters and words scattered across the floor. Try as he might he could not piece together a story. Truth be told he could barely piece together sentences that held any meaning, let alone a story. He was not one to give up at the first hurdle but everything seemed to be against him. In his darker moments he had even begun to think that sinister moves were afoot to prevent him from achieving his goal, from making his mark in the world, from writing his very own book.

His suspicions were correct. From all sides action was being taken. The villagers of Safe Haven led by Samuel, and aided and abetted by Peter and Letitia, would stop at nothing to return the book to how it should be, and steadfastly refused to allow a new, wholly unoriginal, book to be written. They did not fight a lone battle though. Alongside them, fiercely protective of the book, stood noble words and true, letters of character, sentences that denoted bravery and high expectations. The words were fighting back.

Samuel arrived late in the book that evening. He had spent several hours deep in discussion with Alexander. Their numbers were growing…….. On their side they had all the inhabitants of Safe Haven Village, including Peter and Letitia, not to mention

Matthias, the shadow-less figure who had become the unwitting centre of everyone's attention. And now, joining forces with them, came Alexander. For the thief was not only jeopardising the future of the book that Samuel held so dear, he was also waging war on all books, on the world of words. It could not be allowed to happen.

Every time a letter or word was stolen from the book, a little more of storyland was lost. Sometimes a word was stolen just as it was about to be uttered by a parent reading a story to their child. The child would turn and look in surprise at their father or mother, wondering why the words had suddenly died. They could not understand why the story had stopped in mid-sentence. Despite their pleadings for the reading to continue, the parent was not able to do so as the story had stopped. As the sentence was broken so was the story.

The tears of children denied their bedtime story fell throughout the land, and with the tears came sadness and dismay, broken hearts that could not be mended. It was as if a cloak of despair had fallen over all things good and right about their lives, both within the books and outside them. Things must be fixed and all was being taken in hand by the band of those who chose to fight back. Throughout all they did, in their efforts to retrieve the stolen words, ran the words long spoken since ancient times. 'All that is needed for evil to triumph is for good men to do nothing.' No edict ever rang so true, or was so relevant to their cause, as this one.

They gathered in the book at Peter's house as the clock struck seven. Alexander accompanied Samuel and Matthias had been invited by Peter and Letitia. A small, but meaningful, group whose combined knowledge and ideas would surely triumph over the thief. It had to. The alternative did not bear thinking about. A world without stories, devoid of books, totally lacking in make-believe. No escape from the real world to a world of dreams where anything was possible, the only limit being your own imagination.

They set a trap for the thief. It was a trap made from words. The words had been laid on a previously blank page and stacked high in helter-skelter fashion. They were piled in such a way that the thief would be most tempted by the words at the bottom, with those above being cleverly disguised by brushwood and cunning.

A cursory glance would not instantly reveal the pile of words, only those at the bottom. They were hoping against hope that the thief would try to prise away the most valued word at the bottom, the word that spelled 'GOLD'. Even though the thief only needed words to write his own book he was not without greed. When he saw gold he would not be able to resist temptation. As he struggled to claim the word for his own all the words piled high above would unbalance and would cascade down, trapping him. He would be encased in a cage of words.

While he was recovering they would grab him and take him away. First he would be put in the village prison, then he would be put on trial. The group of plotters lay in wait and held their breaths as the night drew on and the shadows began to close in, one of the shadows hopefully being the thief, the shadow of Matthias.

They did not have long to wait. As the minute hand of the clock shifted position, and swung to register half past seven of the hour, the thief's shadow glanced across the page. He paused as his eyes caught sight of the word that shone out from the page, 'GOLD'. He was about to reach for it with outstretched hands when something stopped him dead in his tracks. This was not his gold to take. It did not belong to him. None of it did. These letters and words belonged to no-one. They formed the lives of the story book characters and belonged only to themselves. He hung his head in guilt and shame. How could he have done this? Pursued such an unworthy cause, strayed from the path of goodness, become a power for evil in the world?

'Please forgive me,' he said to the book and looked to the sky where the moon looked down on him. 'I must put things right,' he murmured to himself. 'I will return all the words and letters to their rightful place. I will make the book whole again. I must find the body that I belong to.'

The little group, waiting silently in the bushes, could hardly believe what they were hearing. The shadow was going to redeem himself and become united with Matthias. All would be well. The trap of words had not been needed. Matthias was thankful beyond words and tears ran down his face. He called to his shadow from his hiding place.

'Shadow. I am here. Come to me, I will help you right the wrongs you have done. You will not be punished as you had a change of heart. You are to be admired for your strength of spirit and your decision to put things right.'

As Matthias finished speaking, the shadow raced to his side and blended into Matthias. And with the merging came the knowledge of where all the stolen characters had been hidden. Before the night was over every single lost item had been recovered and replaced in the correct position on the page from where it had been taken. There was much revelry in the book that night, and indeed in many books across the land. Smiles appeared again on the faces of the children, no longer deprived of their bedtime story.

The world of dreams was once more restored to their lives and happiness reigned supreme.

****

As Samuel climbed out of the book the next morning he was exhausted beyond belief. His mother greeted him at the breakfast table:

'Come on sleepy head, you've got a busy day ahead of you. You've done nothing all night except sleep so you should be fresh and ready to tackle all the day has to offer you.' If only she had known the truth……

Thanks very much indeed to Paul, my husband, for taking such care and attention reading through the first draft of Samuel and the Stolen Words. Your patience and support is much appreciated, as always.

Also, I would not be on this pathway of writing books were it not for the presence in my life, for nearly 40 years, of my great friend and author, Ged Neary. You might have left us now Ged but you are not forgotten.